MW01200101

BOB'S DINER

BOB'S DINER

ELLEN T. LEEDS

ILLUSTRATIONS BY ELLEN T. LEEDS

All Illustrations and Cover Art by
Ellen T. Leeds

Book design by Robert Gardner

Independently published by Desert Wind Press LLC

ISBN: 978-1-956271-14-0 (paperback)
ISBN: 978-1-956271-15-7 (eBook)

Dedication

For Danni and Bea Leeds, my parents, who inspired me with their lust for living. And for my husband Zooey, son Leo and his beautiful wife Amy, all who continue to bring joy into my life.

Contents

Fall

Winter

Spring

Summer

And After

Acknowledgments

The author wishes to thank all those encouraging her along her journey to the completion of Bob's Diner. Her three writing teachers George Wendell, Eric Selby and Jeannie DeQuine. Her fellow authors/classmates at the Osher Learning Center on the University of Miami campus, in her many writing classes; especially The Sunshine Writer's Group. Her weekly Zoom writer's group, The Winning Writers, Rose White, Ivy Ames and Zooey Kaplowitz, who pushed her along as they listened to her numerous revisions. Karina Taylee, her patient and kind editor. Robert Gardner, the publisher of Desert Wind Press, who has given his guidance and expertise in bringing Bob's Diner book design clarity and beauty. Her nonconformist parents Danni and Bea Leeds. Her son Leo, who likes to roll his eyes a lot, but nevertheless, is there whenever needed. Finally, her understanding husband Zooey, who has been there through every second of every moment, when she thought she would give up and didn't.

Chapter 1

Bob's Diner Begins

Bob didn't enjoy turning the key of his diner and leaving; he'd much prefer turning the key and entering. He'd prefer to open its doors and begin the day. Like the minute hand on the big clock in Woodlake town's center, one could set their watches by the opening of Bob's Diner. Five o'clock every morning Bob would walk the three blocks to the rear of his beloved diner. It was a quiet, solitary stroll up Clifton to Monmouth, turn left at the Strand Movie Theater, pass the elementary, junior and high schools before rounding the corner and see his diner. He'd check the mailbox, check that the garbage was taken, turn the back door key, and exactly at five eighteen had turned on the kitchen lights, and put four urns of coffee onto the large counter nearest the kitchen pass through.

Next, Bob would make sure to go out front to take the stack of newspapers delivered every day, bring them inside, read the headlines of the Woodlake Gazette, and place the pile next to the cash register upfront by the entrance. He would start getting the baskets of eggs lined up, the bread, and put several large skillets on the burners.

As precisely as all of this was underway, Rosaline the number one waitress at Bob's Diner, was looking out her window to check to see if she'd need an umbrella or not, a sweater or not, and as she drank her eye-opening large glass of orange juice, she began to finish up her preparations before arriving at six to Bob's. In over twenty years had she hardly missed a day of work.

The diner was her home, and Bob and his wife Lilly were her family. She had made a seamless transition from working part-time through high school, to becoming a full-time employee. Her happiest moments were serving the many Woodlake men, women and children who came day in and day out. Lilly, Bob's wife, wasn't a daily fixture. On weekends she usually was tending to the register, but during the week she might or might not show, for she had to attend to their home and keeping it running as Bob did for the Diner.

To assist on the floor was Ginger, and as customers came and went Rosaline and Ginger would take care of the customer's checks. Newspapers, gum, and the like were paid for on an honor system with a big glass bowl that was next to the register. If people in Woodlake were unable to pay their checks due to unforeseen emergencies, they always returned to pay their checks and leave generous tips for Rosaline and Ginger. To Bob, each person entering the doors of his beloved diner were family. Yes, Lilly was family, but his customers were what kept him going and gave him a reason to get up each day. He felt compelled to do his job, because they needed him and he needed them.

The diner was the hub of this community in this New Jersey town. A meeting place for folks. Those waiting to meet someone coming off the bus from the city, or those waiting to venture into the city. Kids dropped off after sport's practice to grab a shake. Teens making clandestine meetings with someone they thought might change their lives forever. Friends catching up and those too lonely just wanting a place to be with others if only for an hour or so. Within its memorabilia covered walls, people connected and belonged. It belonged to them in heart as much as to Bob. This is Bob's Diner and these are its stories.

Chapter 2

Chocolate Cake

This was Rosaline's 38th Birthday. Again, she was sitting alone in Bob's Diner. Sitting alone for her birthday. She had no true friends, with the exception of Bob n' Lilly. Once a year she'd have her birthday dinner at Bob's Diner.

Time for Rosaline had stopped the day her mother said, "I love you very much; but I gotta go, I can't stay in this town one more second. Rosaline, today you turned 18 and I know you can make it on your own." Out the door, Rosaline watched as her mother walked down the street carrying a brown well-worn suitcase covered in travel stickers. She jumped into a blue Ford pick-up truck with a tall stranger in faded overalls driving; except for an occasional call, was never seen again.

Never had a birthday gone by for Rosaline without a freshly baked New Jersey apple pie, bought at the local A&P supermarket, being front and center. The last birthday pie that Roseline's mom ever gave her was an apple pie, with lightly dusted sugar on top for her 18th birthday. She served the pie, kissed her daughter tenderly on the cheek, picked up her coat, suitcase and disappeared. That was twenty years ago. They had eaten it that day at the kitchen table and before she knew it, Rosaline's life as she had lived it before was over.

Bob knew it was Rosaline's birthday, "Another birthday Roz? I guess I'll go get you the usual," and before Rosaline got a chance to answer, Bob was off to the kitchen.

Every week was the same for Rosaline. After she left work, she'd walk home and sit in front of the TV with a Swanson TV dinner on a wobbly metal tray with painted faded flowers. On Fridays, after work, Bob would serve her his blue-plate special: a cup of split pea soup, Salisbury steak, mashed potatoes, and rice pudding.

Once a year for her birthday, Rosaline deviated. She would splurge and have the Prime Rib Special: Caesar salad with blue cheese dressing, a baked potato, and a huge slice of apple pie with a vanilla ice cream topping, as an added birthday bonus. Funny though, apple pie was never her favorite. She secretly delighted in thinking of a seven-layer chocolate cake, edged in white and red flowers, with twinkling birthday candles. Just thinking about the gooey chocolate cake made her feel disloyal, somehow. Her mother must have known it wasn't Rosaline's favorite, and yet she always served her an apple pie every year, on her birthday.

Rosaline never dared change from the pattern of her life. She hoped that if she kept things just as her mother liked them, her mother would return.

"Hello, Roz, I am in California. It is so beautiful out here. Did I miss your birthday again? So sorry. I hope you had a slice of apple pie to celebrate. Maybe we will get together again soon. It's so hot out here. I am glad you are doing well. The plane tickets are very expensive these days." Before Rosaline could get a word out, her mother would say, "I gotta go."

The calls from Rosaline's mom were always sporadic and abrupt. There was never a word asking Rosaline about her life. Maybe it was better that way, for Rosaline didn't know how she'd answer that question.

"How was my life," she thought as she stared out the diner's windows plastered with posters, lit by the flashing light outside saying, OPEN. "My life? It's the same. I'm turning thirty-eight and nothing has changed," Rosaline ruminated. "I am alone when I climb into bed at night. My phone never rings and I'm afraid that I will always be alone." Her thoughts were interrupted by the crashing sound of a plate as it hit the table. Bob was slapping the salad, prime rib, and baked potato in front of her. Bits of salad flipped into the air and the baked potato almost slid off as Rosaline quickly caught it before it reached her lap. Between rushing in and out of the kitchen, Bob asked, "Are you ok?" "Am I ok?" Rosaline was caught off guard by that question. "Am I Ok," she screamed at Bob who charged back into the kitchen. Surely, Bob didn't really want to know, because before she was able to respond, he disappeared, and just as quickly she heard the clanging of the counter bell Bob was pounding on, signaling a food pickup for Ginger.

Again, alone Rosaline decided to respond in her head, "I am not Ok, and I am not too good. In fact, my life is awful. I am sitting here in this diner, eating alone on my 38th birthday. Eating the same Caesar salad, the same prime rib, and the same baked potato that I have done for almost 20 years! Nothing is good about my life! Absolutely nothing! "

No one deeply cared if she was ok. Friends like Bob n' Lilly cared for her, but if she didn't start caring about her own life, and begin loving the true Rosaline, no one special would either. It was at that moment, an internal switch signaled her, that Rosaline knew. Forty was nearing her soul. In two years, she'd be forty and her deepest understanding screamed out! Her mother was never coming back. If she continued to eat the apple pie or not, no one cared. "I better start caring," she thought. She had always despised having apple pie on her birthday!!!! As Bob rounded the corner with the biggest slice of apple pie that she had ever seen, she knew hands down.

As Rosaline momentarily reached for her fork, she put it down. She leaped uncharacteristically out of her seat and stood akimbo in front of Bob, "NO, not today! Bring me a slice of that chocolate cake," she said, pointing to the glass spinning cake display next to the counter, "Please, better yet; bring me the entire cake! I don't want that apple pie! Not today, not tomorrow, not ever!" Bob nearly fell off his heals, spun around and vaulted back to the kitchen disposing of the apple pie. "Hey, Bob," she blasted for everyone to hear, "One big, CHOCOLATE CAKE. And if there are any birthday candles in the back, I'd like those, too!"

Rosaline delighted in helping to finish almost every piece of that ginormous chocolate cake. She had invited Bob and Ginger to sit down and join her. Each tangy bite pleased her. Rosaline understood that no longer having the apple pie wasn't the only thing that needed to be changed. From here on lots of changes were going to happen and she would have to be the catalyst for those changes.

As the noise from the booth rang out, all patrons turned for they couldn't avoid hearing Rosaline's boisterous laughter. "I need more napkins," as the soft creamy icing dripped down her face. "Wow, how did we manage to eat that entire cake? I think I'd like to wash it down with a tall glass of Coca Cola, please!" Bob, Ginger and Rosaline were stuffed. They talked into the night.

The sweetness of the flavorful chocolate stayed on Rosaline's lips for a very long time. She savored that moment. As the yummy taste lingered in her mouth, Roz knew for a fact, things would never be the same again, and that was a good thing, a very good thing!

Chapter 3

Mr. Twitters

M r. Twitters was about five-foot-tall, maybe four foot nine. No one knew because no one ever asked him. He came into Bob's Diner every Thursday and ordered a coffee, no milk and toast buttered lightly on both sides. He would sit at the counter and read the diner's menu with great intent, but since he always left soon after finishing his toast and never ate lunch or dinner, one might wonder why he studied the menu so thoroughly. He always wore a bright red jacket that was zipped up the front, brown khaki pants, and well-worn brown hiking boots. It was hard to guess his age, but possibly in his forties. His tousled hair had light grey streaks. He always paid in cash and left the waitress a 15-cent tip.

Bob's Diner was on the south side of town, and students and teachers would come by lunch time, or later in the evening for burgers, fries, and shakes. The only high school in town was two blocks away, and other than the school cafeteria, this was it.

Roseline would often sit down in the booths with customers and schmooze. Rosaline had worked at Bob's far too many years to count, and she knew most of the customers by name. "Mary, that's a special blouse you've got on today." "Buzz, I heard that there was an infestation of beetles devouring Lillian's pink hydrangeas!" Before, the customer could utter a word in response, Rosaline floated over to the next booth.

Mr. Twitters was one of her customers who was rather mysterious. He never looked up, never made any eye contact. Her thoughts of being with someone kept flooding her mind. Here was a curious quiet man that might be available.

"If I don't speak up, perhaps I'll never get another chance," she spoke deliberately to herself. Her internal voice continued to become louder crowding out her fears. Although, Rosaline, didn't know his name, she one day, with strong intent, boldly asked him, "What's your name?" and he said, "Mr. Twitters," and went straight back to reading the menu. Rosaline was expecting more from this odd man, but she believed this was a beginning. She now knew he had a name.

Bob's Diner was Rosaline's Valhalla. She was the queen of the diner. Ever since she graduated from high school, she worked full time in Bob's. Her aspirations at one time were to be the fastest typist in the east, but she never could get beyond 25 words per minute, no matter how hard she tried. Working in Bob's was her safe haven.

She had always been large and gawky with one leg slightly longer than the other, due to the fact that her mother accidentally ran over it at an early age with the family station wagon. When she walked her body shifted up and down and left and right, but that never diminished her huge smile, and humungous hugs she frequently gave the customers when they had good news or sad news to share. The high school boys loved being enveloped into her robust bosom.

She always tried blending into the walls when she was young and attended high school. Her hair was brown, wild, and curly, not straight, and blond and she never learned how to control it. High school was a place to fit in with the "right group," the cheerleaders, the brains, the jocks, and "pretty ones who often put out," -- she was none of those. But when she walked through the doors of Bob's, all that hurt, and torment was left behind. She was part of a family, although she always wanted her own, she tried not to dwell on it ever happening, until the strange, and intriguing Mr. Twitters sat at her counter.

Rosaline was about to engage Mr. Twitters in further conversation, as she had with many other customers that day, but at that exact moment, he put the fifteen cents on the counter and left. Rosaline watched him walk toward the door, and noticed he was carrying what looked like a briefcase, and he was swinging it back and forth.

Mr. Twitters was gone for several weeks, and Rosaline thought about where he had gone, and what he did for a living. Did he have a wife, family? Had Mr. Twitters ever thought about her? Random thoughts about customers often crossed Rosaline's mind, but never as much as those about Mr. Twitters. She loved playing these mind games about people. What did they do at night? Were they happy? Did they travel to faraway places?

For the next two weeks Rosaline played this game in her head. Every time the luncheonette doors swung open, she would try to guess if Mr. Twitters would be coming through them. After graduating high school, she had always hoped someone would come through the doors of Bob's to sweep her off her wobbling feet. After almost twenty years had come and gone, she had almost stopped believing, but not completely. Her hopeless optimism still reared its head, and it couldn't stop her from looking at the door every Thursday for a glance, per chance, of seeing Mr. Twitters.

Thursdays came and went, but finally, on that particular Thursday, in he walked, sat at the counter and asked for his usual, coffee black, and toast buttered on both sides. For some unknown reason, Rosaline having reviewed this moment over and over, blurted out to Mr. Twitters if he was married. Mr. Twitters looked up from his coffee, and simply said, "No." That was the correct answer, Rosaline thought.

Rosaline then charged ahead, "Would you like to have dinner with me some evening?"

She had also thought of that question for months, thought of asking him many times, and today was the day.

"Mrs. Twitters," she had reviewed the sound of that in her head. How easily the two parts went together. She might be a bit overweight, she might not know how to type, but she could make mean scrambled eggs, and an amazing, fabulous melted grilled cheese sandwich. Watching Bob over the years had made her an ace in the kitchen. Yes, Mrs. Twitters sounded very good in her head.

-- M.R.S. T.W.I.T.T.E.R.S.-- spelling each letter out carefully in her mind. Perhaps she was getting ahead of herself.

She was about to repeat her invitation, thinking perhaps he hadn't heard her, but quietly, and without looking up, Mr. Twitters said, "Yes."

Rosaline was not sure if Mr. Twitters knew her name, but that would come. She was not sure if he knew she was almost 5 foot nine. She was not sure of anything. But one thing she was sure of, he had said, "Yes." "Meet me here tonight at six," she rapidly fired back. And with that Mr. Twitters left his usual fifteen cents on the counter. He turned to leave quickly through the doors. He made sure to face forward hiding his tears of joy and fear rolling down his face.

It was without question, without an inkling of doubt, that Rosaline positively heard him say, in an ever so low whisper … "OK. I'll meet you at six."

Chapter 4

The Disappearance of Toby's Bike

Geese flapping their wings and landing onto Woodlake's lake as leaves were beginning to turn bright colors of orange and red. Squirrels chasing each other up the tall pine branches circling round and round seeming to want to attach onto or grab each other's tails. Pine cones dropping on the ground, as ducks quacked at one another gently gliding through the still water. Children swinging nearby and laughing as they pumped their legs back and forth trying to reach higher and higher into the cool October air of New Jersey.

Toby had peddled her bike for blocks and blocks and was delighted to be at the lakes edge to watch the birds searching for food, and she had a bag of bread exactly for that purpose. She gently lay her bike down on the soft grass nearby and began throwing the crumbs into the glassy water. As she thrust each handful, groups of ducks jostled for positions to get a taste of the delicious morsels. Several geese pushed into the crowd and squawked to get their fair share. This was Toby's weekly ritual and she often wondered if they scheduled an appearance knowing she'd be there.

Unfortunately, on this Friday afternoon John DeCosta also knew Toby's routine and as she was happily feeding the ducks and geese. He decided after pondering this for many a week, that her pristine, sparkling blue bike, with white streamers attached to the handles, would become his. He picked it off the ground and before Toby was aware of its disappearance, he peddled away.

At last, after perhaps close to an hour of feeding and watching the geese fly off in a v-formation, Toby turned around walking to where she had left her Schwinn bike, and it was no longer there. She thought that perhaps someone had placed it somewhere else, so as not to trip over it, but no it was gone, just plain gone. She hadn't seen anyone watching her, and she couldn't think of anyone in Woodlake who would take her bike, but she knew it just couldn't have vanished. What would her parents say? She knew she'd better find it before they found out.

She wasn't sure of the time, but today her mom was meeting her at Bob's diner for lunch, so without her wheels she knew she better start walking quickly. Toby's bike was her freedom and escape. She loved traveling the streets of Woodlake. When it had rained, going through puddles was such fun, and now in the fall the leaves made crunchy noises as the bike's tires weaved in and out of the piles raked along the driveways. Her mom would know something was wrong. Toby could never hide anything from her mom.

It hummed through her head as she walked the leaf covered streets, that someone didn't like her, and so much so that they had stolen her most prized possession. She'd find a penny in the street and wonder who had lost it. She'd always run after a friend if they left their sweater on the seat after class. It was beyond her thinking and heart that such a person was in the world who could take that which wasn't theirs.

Her mind immediately thought that perhaps whoever had taken it might have mistaken it for their bike, but no that wasn't possible. Her Schwinn had white streamers on the blue bike, and it had been special ordered by her dad for her birthday because the store only sold ones with pink streamers, and she wanted to have her school colors. Maybe there had been an emergency and they had planned on only borrowing it for a little while, and it would return shortly. Toby so much wanted the world to be good, but today it wasn't very easy.

The diner was only several blocks away and as she neared it her heart began to beat so fast. *"I've got to tell my mom",* *she thought.* It was the worst thing in her recent life that she had to confess to her mother: someone, a bad person, had deliberately taken her bike. It wasn't but five minutes as Toby pushed the double doors to the diner open, she blurted out, "My bike. It's gone. I turned around to feed the ducks and when I looked back it was gone. Gone." Toby repeated those words over and over. Tears were forming in the corner of her eyes and flooding her face, "I can't believe that my bike is gone, who would do such a thing?" Her mom enveloped her into her arms and said, "Don't worry, maybe we will find it. Calm down." But it was no use, Toby just couldn't stop the tears from pouring down her face.

Rosaline came by and placed a large chocolate shake on the table to see if that might squelch the hurt, and Bob prepared the largest dish of crisp French fries that anyone had ever seen. Soon the food made some of Toby's pain dissipate, but she couldn't stop thinking about her favorite possession vanishing.

On the other side of town, John DeCosta was driving his newly acquired wheels up and down his driveway. No one was home, as was usual. His mother would see him off in the mornings with a quick breakfast, and his dad was rarely ever there. When his dad was home there was always lots of fighting, drinking and screaming, so when he was gone everyone was happy. By the time his mother returned home, John usually had fallen asleep on the couch eating the sandwich left for him in the kitchen. "Hey what do you think of my new bike?" he spoke to no one, and no one answered.

Some nights John DeCosta would wait up hoping that his mom would be there before he went to sleep, but other than the mornings when she prepared his breakfast, he was alone. His dirty laundry was taken care of, there was always an extra sandwich in the kitchen for him when he came home, his sheets on his bed were changed weekly, but his mother was almost like a phantom. Once he had asked her if he could move in with his grandmother who lived in the next county over, and she looked at him and said, "Oh, she died three months ago." He didn't know if that was so. He made sure to go to school, so that no one would come looking for him, and no one ever did.

The novelty of the bike soon wore off for John DeCosta. His mother never questioned how he got the bike, even though he had left it in the driveway several days, and she had to step over it to enter the house. No one in the neighborhood cared either. Finally, late one Sunday afternoon John DeCosta drove it over to Bob's diner and left it near the front door.

Eventually, Bob spotted the bike and looked around but saw no one nearby. He knew it was Toby's because she spoke of its white streamers and called Toby's mother, who said she'd come right over to pick it up.

"Who left it here? I'd love to thank them. Wait till Toby sees it," Toby's exuberant mom said.

Toby was overjoyed to have her bike back, and she often wondered who had taken her bike, and who had brought it back.

John DeCosta recently wondered who had taken his mom, because one day she was gone and never returned. He hadn't seen any signs of her for several days. His mom, desperate and overwhelmed with the raising of her son while trying to keep her job, merely surviving; had disappeared into the sea of humanity.

His dad showed up, moved him to the next county over to live with his grandmother who hadn't died.

Toby left wondering about who had taken her bike, and John DeCosta left wondering who had taken his mom.

And as things sometimes go in life----

Neither of them ever found out.

Chapter 5

Nathan Twitters Returns

The bus pulled up to the station and Nathan Twitters stared out of its dirty windows. His dreams of getting away from the dreary small-town life of Woodlake and moving to the rumblings of New York City had been shattered. In New York City, he could reinvent himself. In Woodlake everyone knew everything about everyone. He could barely make out the people standing outside waiting for family or friends to depart. He took his hand and wiped the steam and soot off with his palm. It said Woodlake on the platform, and as he stood up to get his briefcase from the overhead rack, he wondered how this could possibly be.

He had everything mapped out: moving away from home to go to college, find a job in the city, and leave this small-town life behind. It had been almost a year of going from odd job to odd job when he read in his hometown paper, that his mother religiously sent him, that Woodlake High School was advertising for a history teacher. His mother had made it a point to circle the ad in bright red crayon, and call him way too often, to remind him that this was an opportunity too good to pass up. He reluctantly sent in his resume, and since the principal knew Nathan, he hired him without even an interview.

He hadn't told his overbearing mother he was returning today to avoid her, "I Told You So's." He rented a small apartment over The Spot's candy store, and stepped off the bus, got his suitcase brought from below by the bus driver, and proceeded to walk the five blocks to The Spot. The sky was blue and showed no movement. It was a normal hot New Jersey summer, and the five blocks seemed to stretch on for miles. School wouldn't be starting for another month.

Twenty years later Nathan was still living over The Spot in his small but bare apartment. He had the necessities. Everything was almost as he had found it. There was a square folding card table with two wooden folding chairs, an overstuffed easy chair, a bed, and a dresser. All things left from the previous renters.

The only changes were a current calendar on a nail in the kitchen that he received for free every year from the current mayor of Woodlake. He had added on the living room wall, with scotch tape, unframed, The Look Magazine cover of President Kennedy. Two untouched phone books, the yellow and white pages, were stacked near the entrance door.

He never had visitors and only once had his mother come to see where he lived. She had found it very hard to climb three flights up and three flights down, and after barely able to catch her breath, she never returned. That was perfectly fine with Nathan.

Yet, after visiting Bob's diner every Thursday for months upon months and getting to watch Rosaline bring platters of food to its many patrons, and his own toast buttered on both sides; she had asked him to join her for dinner. Nathan had no idea what he would say or do alone with Rosaline.

Why, after all these years, did he finally decide to chance his solitary life? Why did he turn right instead of left? He had no trouble lecturing to his students about the Civil War, or George Washington, but when it came to making friends or chatting in the teacher's lounge, it was all too painful. He made sure to never turn in late lesson plans, always had his grades in on time, and followed every rule in the Woodlake Teacher's Handbook. Nathan did not want to cause problems or be singled out for any mishaps.

Somehow that number forty-three approaching made him think about the next twenty years. Except for his mother, who he reluctantly had dinner with once a week, there was no one. His weekly dinners with his mother were oppressive. She did the talking, and the questioning. "Nathan, how is your job? Have you made any friends? I bet you heard that Toby's bike was stolen and returned." She'd drone on with the same conversation each time they were together. He had listened to the same stories and his brain had begun to go on overload.

It appeared he had managed to learn to live with the stares, and whispers. "Oh, you know that Nathan Twitters, he is a loner. An odd little man. A strange one that Twitters." Yet, lately he was beginning to feel uncomfortable.

He never questioned his life, his choices, but as the humidity rolled into Woodlake, something didn't sit right. He looked at his blue shirts lined up in his closet and picked out the newest one. He had over a dozen shirts. Everyone the same. He zipped up his red jacket and headed to Bob's Diner to meet Rosaline. "I don't know if I can do this. I have nothing to offer and she'll hate me," Nathan repeated and repeated, "I have nothing to offer, absolutely nothing."

Rosaline wasn't sure what this evening was going to be. She had friends and had found a home and family in Bob's Diner. The kids and teenagers, her daily regulars, Bob n' Lilly, so many that made her smile each day. Yet, when she left for the day, walked to her home, turned the key, only her cat was there to greet her. Sarah, her beloved cat, was comforting, but that was no longer enough. A relationship for herself was never ever going to happen, until Mr. Twitters became a possibility.

She had led a life filtered through observing the events of others. She observed each fiber of other people's daily existence, and her own was put on a shelf. Other people were meant to fall in love; but not her.

She asked Bob for a couple of hours to go home and get ready. She hoped that the pink flowered dress that she had worn for Bob n' Lilly's wedding still fit. She still had the pearls her mother gave her on her sixteenth birthday with the matching button earrings. She knew for sure that she would have to wear her white waitress shoes because her feet always were swollen after standing on them for so many hours at Bob's, and that would be fine.

She'd never ever had been on a date. Hard to believe that someone her age never got asked out, but it was so.

Rosaline stood and looked at herself in the mirror. The dress gapped at the bust line, but she was able to adjust her white shawl to cover it. She adjusted the pearls, and took the bobby pins out of her hair. Aside from when she took showers or slept, Rosaline never let her hair cascade down. She looked at the clock and knew that Mr. Twitters would be at the diner in fifteen minutes. She adjusted her slip, took one last look in the mirror, and began what she believed was to be her most important walk to Bob's Diner.

Yet, Rosaline waited and waited and Nathan never showed up.

"As I expected," tears dotting her eyes. "As I expected," she repeated over and over, "As I expected."

Chapter 6

Toby's Field Day

"Ok, the next person picked, Gail over on this side," shouted Carmen Thompson, the gym teacher with her silver whistle tangling and glistening in the sun. Gail happily ran to Team ones' line and stood awaiting the softball game to begin. It was a crisp September day. Labor Day was over and school had begun several weeks ago after a long lazy summer. Physical education classes at Woodlake Junior High were a daily routine on the schedule.

Everyone had to have their blue gym uniforms inspected, white socks and white Keds sneakers were all part of the routine. Aside from Toby never wanting to be playing baseball, the gym uniforms were an added unflattering addition to this dreadful experience. The elastic bands around the legs cut into her thighs, and although she was just in junior high school her large breasts made the snaps in the chest area forever popping open. It was embarrassing to her. One humiliating thing after another.

"Jane, you are picked for Team two," Mrs. Thompson continued. Another sigh of relief that she was chosen and not left for last. Everyone knew that those picked last were the girls no one truly wanted. Every girl had to be picked because Mrs. Thompson made sure to give the speech about sportsmanship, and fairness. She also emphasized, "Someone has to be picked last, that's how nature works, but ladies that is no indication of how you are as a player. We must be good sports and above all be kind to one another." Of course, all the girls knew deep down in their souls what she was saying had no shred of truth in it, yet they stood and shook their heads in full agreement. It was bad enough having to march outside for all the boys to point and see those dreadful uniforms that pulled tightly with its cinched belt, that Toby could never get around her tummy; but then to stand in the hot sun and wait to be picked for a baseball game that she wanted no part of to begin with was almost unbearable.

"Becky Team One, hurry up we only have an hour. Stop primping and come here."

Becky forever pushing back her wavy blond hair, and somehow always looking fabulous in those ugly uniforms. For some unknown reason, there were those girls who looked good, even if they were to wear a brown paper bag.

There was that time, during the class play on vegetables, third grade Toby thought, where Becky played a sack of potatoes and could have won the Miss Junior Miss contest dressed that way. Nothing ever looked bad on Becky. She would only need to flash those long eyelashes over and over, give her white sparkling toothy grin while tilting her head to the side and the judges would get overpowered by her cuteness.

"Lynn team one," and back and forth it went until only Toby and Jane were standing to be chosen. "Oh, no please let Jane be last. I don't want to be known as that girl," Toby thought, but the outcome was as she suspected, last again. Toby ambled quietly over to her team captain who graciously shook her hand as a welcome gesture, that Toby knew to be so unwelcoming with all the other girls staring and knowing the truth.

She then took her spot in the outfield which was so far out that for most of the hour remaining she would just stand there because none of the girls ever hit a ball that far. She had always hated being in this position and wondered why such torture was inflicted on her every year. "Some girls were just born athletes", she thought. She totally believed this and that others like herself were better at other things. What exactly she and others were better at was still a total mystery to her.

"Toby run in. The ball is headed your way, run, run catch it!" she was awoken from her daydream by screams from her team members. "Catch it, Toby. Run, Toby run!" The girls on her team continued shouting and screaming but the ball was nowhere in her vision. By the time she saw it coming it smacked her right in her forehead and she fell to the ground. Mrs. Thompson came running onto to the field and helped Toby off the field and told her to go see the school nurse immediately. Not only was she last to be picked but now all eyes were on her as she sauntered away. The pain began to throb, but Toby was more humiliated than in pain. She wished she could just be invisible and disappear.

Inside the building in the principal's office was the school nurse, who with a smile for Toby, made her lie down on the cot. The cot was covered with a starched, crisp white sheet and a pillow where Toby tried resting. The small nurses' office was covered with safety posters, Give to the Red Cross. Smokey Bear proclaiming, Only you can prevent forest fires, and one heralding Help Eradicate Polio with a small tearful child waiting for her turn to see the doctor. There was a mobile of wooden parakeets perched on circular wires hanging over the cot, and a few glass bottles filled with Band-Aids, tongue depressors and another with cotton balls.

"Why that's a big knot you have on your forehead. Don't move it needs an ice bag and a lollipop," Miss Katie, the school nurse said. Toby winced as the cold ice bag was placed on her temple. Toby pleaded, "Please, don't make me go out there again, can you write me a note for the rest of the year? Please! I hate it. Sports are dangerous. Sports are not for everyone, and especially not me!"

"Won't be for the rest of the year but at least until tomorrow," Nurse Katie chuckled back at Toby. "I am going to telephone your mother to come take you home for the rest of the day. I think that bump needs to go down a bit and you'd be more comfortable in your own bed." This indeed pleased Toby at least she wouldn't have to face those girls for a while.

When Toby's mother showed up, she was told by the Nurse Katie that along with the lollipop, more ice and a large shake at Bob's Diner before heading home might be the best medicine for a swift recovery. Toby's mother, never wanting to disobey doctor's or nurse's orders, took Toby to Bob's where he made her the biggest chocolate shake with lots of whip cream and a huge cherry on top prepared especially for her. This somehow made Toby's pain disappear even for just a little while.

Toby chose to not think about that now and slurped her shake down to the very, very bottom. A mother's hug, and a huge chocolate shake somehow was all she needed until tomorrow!

Chapter 7

Roseline Escapes

Rosaline was tired. Flat out tired. Tired of the people and the diner and most of all- the routine. Up at six, jump in the shower, put on stockings, her white comfort shoes, her uniform, and eat her usual breakfast of a bowl of cereal, toast and glass of orange juice. She checked the clock on her kitchen wall and never left the house before 6:46 AM. She would walk the five blocks to Bob's and be there before seven.

Why the malaise had been drowning her today, was unclear. She never felt tired. She was the perky one. The waitress with the smile. Yet, on her walk to Bob's the heaviness that lay on her shoulders stuck. She felt weighed down by loneliness, although she was surrounded by those who cared about her. It was not enough. She yearned for someone to go to sleep with at night and wake up with in the morning.

She had anticipated Mr. Twitters returning for their rendezvous. She had thought about him taking her out for a dinner in the neighboring town, but it had been weeks and no Mr. Twitters. She had waited and waited on the diner's steps, anticipating his appearance, and he never came or called. He vanished. She was sure he was going to show up. What had she done wrong?

She knew all the rhetoric about patience and taking things as they come, but it was years of waiting and countless disappointments. How many smiles would it take to make someone interested in the true Rosaline, the real Rosaline?

It was the beginning of the week, and as she entered the diner, she only saw Bob reading the newspaper. He was slouching over the counter up front, by the cash register instead of his usual spot in the kitchen, peering out. "Hey, Roz, all ok?" he knew her so well and her face spoke volumes. She usually bounced into work, and grinned ear to ear. "Not today," loomed through her head. But, "I'm fine," she mechanically replied out loud.

Bob knew she was anything but fine. Rosaline had worked at the diner since she graduated high school, and today was a rare day for her. She wanted to leave, and that thought had never crossed her mind before.

"Are you sure? Something up with you?" Bob responded. Intuitively he knew something was amiss.

"Can I go home, I think I am not feeling too well," she suddenly blurted out. She wasn't exactly lying, physically ok, but truly not well.

Rosaline's words had stopped him in his tracks. He quickly sputtered, "Yea, sure take the day off. Are you absolutely sure there's nothing I can do?" Before he got the words out, and began walking towards her, she turned and left.

Bob never expected this, not from Rosaline. In her more than twenty years at the diner she had only missed five days of work when her mother passed. It was sudden and the body had to be shipped back from California, where her mother had disappeared, emotionally, decades ago. She didn't truly feel attached to her mom at the time, but as her only relative, Rosaline knew it was her duty. She made all the arrangements, invited the town's people, bought flowers, and wrote a splendid obituary.

Today, rather unexpectedly, Rosaline felt a longing, and a deep sadness bubbling up from within. She rarely thought of how her childhood, and her mother leaving, wounded her. Rosaline always shook off these feelings of longings and aloneness. Yet, today was the exception because Mr. Twitters had rekindled lost hope. Hope to be needed by someone.

She wanted to leave the diner and get away. She wanted to leave the diner before the day had barely begun. The immediacy was pushing her out. She didn't know where she would go at 7:00 AM. The diner was the only place she ever had been to, for over twenty years, at this time of day. It felt unusual, different, strange, and exciting all rolled up into one; tantalizing even.

Maybe walk in the park or go to The Spot for a magazine-- the possibilities seemed endless. She had never altered her routine, never left Bob to fend for himself, never intentionally told a little white lie. It felt a bit scandalous and exhilarating. *Maybe I should work the evening shift, or look for another job? No, that would be too drastic*, Rosaline ruminated. It was freeing enough to have the entire Monday all to herself. She didn't have to decide now. She didn't have to know it all. Crossing the street, she checked the movie schedule at The Strand. She thought that perhaps at three she might actually sit down in the middle of the day, popcorn in hand, and escape.

The word escape felt delicious to Rosaline.

Very delicious indeed.

Chapter 8

Sundays With Nathan

Sitting in the pew on Sunday, as an adult, was comforting for Nathan Twitters. He could be alone and think with minor interruptions from the service. Alone with his thoughts was miraculous. Growing up, Sundays were filled with many interruptions and never any quiet. His mother had high expectations for Sundays. She managed staying out of his life during the week by disappearing into her "soaps", but Sundays were the days to drag Nathan to Woodlake's small but visible nondenominational church. Nathan was forced to wear his blue suit, striped, blue tie, and brown oxfords. The collar was so tight it strangled him, and to make things worse, if it were cold, his parker jacket, gloves, scarf, and woolen hat were never optional.

He was expected to read all the prayers and be engaged. His mother flourished on Sundays as she flaunted her array of flowered hats and garish bright red woolen coat. Into Nathan's quiet, silent inner world came his mother's onslaughts of constant jabbering of whatever might fly through her brain. "Oh, did you hear about…?" or "The Reverend has…. Blah, Blah, Blah." Nathan simply nodded yes or no, which most of the time, allowed him to tune out her endless chatter.

Sitting here today brought back some of the familiarity that Nathan liked while filtering out those not so fond memories. He was thinking about Rosaline. She had some of that forcefulness of his mother, yet he noticed a less demanding side of her. He wasn't sure why he was so afraid to return and see her again. For months he had come every Thursday to the diner just watching her serving customers. He would glance up whenever she went into the kitchen so she wouldn't see his stares. He wasn't sure if she had noticed him.

He had been alone for so many years. His job at the high school was secure and comfortable. Year after year he presented his lectures on the Revolutionary or Civil Wars to the Senior Class. These Seniors knew that if they took copious notes, they would be able to pass his class and graduate. After graduation, like he once thought, they too could leave Woodlake forever.

Those Thursdays brought him great happiness. He had something, someone, to look forward to. He never thought it possible. It was enough to watch Rosaline and wonder in his head what it could be like. There was that one time when he attended college and he was assigned a lab partner in biology. She and Nathan dissected a frog together, but after class was done, he never had the courage to ask her to join him for a cup of coffee. He would fantasize about her, but it faded quickly when he saw her on campus one day walking hand in hand with some boy. Not until he entered Bob's and Rosaline asked for his order did he again risk such thoughts.

The Reverend stepped up and asked everyone to open

to page six. Nathan was happy to just sit there. His small act of defiance was to keep the book and its pages shut. There was no mother force feeding him the scriptures. The choir's singing was calming, and he was able to listen and enjoy the music. The Reverend always invited the entire congregation for punch and cookies, but Nathan managed to give a fast handshake, smile, and head home. He would buy the Sunday paper at The Spot and do the crossword puzzle. He wondered what Rosaline did on her Sundays. She never came to church. Maybe she worked at the diner. Woodlake was so small, but he never saw her on the streets or even at the grocery store. He had agreed to have dinner with her several weeks ago. It just slipped out of his mouth, but what would he say to her? After that, his Thursday mornings had become full of anxiety and so he stopped going to the diner, and never showed for their scheduled meeting. The rest of the week was fine, but he wasn't able to wake up easily on Thursdays anymore. Rosaline's expectations, conversations, and then what? He remembered that girl in biology holding hands with that boy. He never held a woman's hand other than his mothers. He finally admitted that secret to himself. He'd be better off alone, his mind argued with himself.

Nathan had the entire Sunday to himself, and many activities. He had hours ahead to complete the crossword puzzle, he would be able to work in his backyard garden which his landlord had supplied him with, prepare his lunches for the week, and read the funnies. In the backyard, he'd watch the butterflies. Sometimes he planted seeds and other times fiddled with his guitar. He didn't play well, but it helped pass the time. It would be a day of solitude for Nathan.

Yet, while walking home this Sunday afternoon, from deep within, came a decision to turn right instead of left. His heart began racing, and his palms started to sweat. As he neared the Diner, he sat on the steps for a moment tugging on his short red jacket. Beads of water sprang from his temples. His mouth felt dry. At last, he stood, zipped open his jacket, forcefully pushed through the double doors, went directly to his spot at the counter, and as Rosaline approached with her order pad, she was startled by Nathan simply saying, "Sorry, I never followed through with our date, but can I try again? Can we have dinner tonight?" Rosaline wanted to be angry and demanding, yet here he was. She herself knew that change never came easy. She needed to trust Nathan. Seeing him so vulnerable and showing up was exactly the change she had hoped from him.

"Seven, I'll expect you tonight at seven." He said not a word. He shook his head, turned and left.

She briefly watched him go through the diner's swinging front doors before entering the kitchen. She noticed his gait seemed a bit more energized. Her heart was fluttering. He had changed his mind before, so why believe him this time? Somehow, intuitively, she knew, this time, he would return at seven; at seven on the dot.

This time he knew that he was absolutely going to follow through.

He also knew he would absolutely return at seven. At seven on the dot, too.

Chapter 9

Pink Blanket

The solitary movie theater in Woodlake was every kid's hangout on weekends. Parents dropped their children off early Saturday morning and picked them up later that evening. The early hours started out with dozens of cartoons, followed by movie shorts, and finally two features, with one fifteen-minute intermission. The cost was a total of 50 cents for the movies, and 50 cents for refreshments. The noise level in the theater at times was deafening, but no one complained, especially those teens sent along to be the children's chaperons. They were chaperons in name only, because the first chance they got, they usually would sneak up into the balconies to do what teenagers do.

Carmen Thompson was the gym teacher at Woodlake Junior High. She took her job at the junior high school very seriously. She took her parenting very seriously, because after her husband went out for the week-end Sunday edition of the Woodlake News, he never returned. She had to protect her daughter Carmela. She had told her one and only daughter Carmela to keep her legs closed, her hair away from her eyes, and her shoulders back. Carmela always said, "Yes, mother," but as soon as she walked out the door, her legs felt open for action, her rubber band holding her hair away from her face was left undone, and she slouched all the way to her high school's front door. No matter what Carmen tried to instill in her daughter, Carmela felt it her duty, as a teen, to do the opposite. She knew she should have obeyed her mother, but just because….she didn't!

Benny Cohen was the editor of the Woodlake High School Newspaper. He was not only the editor of the high school newspaper, but very good looking. He did have a rather large nose, and huge round eyeglasses, and Carmela was smitten by him. He had brown slicked back hair, and wore brown khaki pants with shiny penny loafers. It was Carmela's Sweet 16 Birthday, and she was allowed to invite boys for the first time. Her mother made sure that she was there to chaperon. It just wouldn't be respectable for Carmela and her friends to be left all alone. Carmela wanted this party to be a hit, so she devised a hair brain scheme to get her mom out of the house, and it worked. She knew that WJH, as the junior high was nick named, could call her mother day or night if there was any kind of emergency and her mom, like Wonder Woman, would save the day. The Woodlake Junior High was Carmen's fortress, and she wouldn't allow anyone or anything to harm it. So, when Fred, the janitor called to say the alarm had gone off, and she had to come immediately to make sure that the building was secure, off she flew leaving Carmela alone. Carmela knew then and there that they had the opportunity to play a quick game of spin the bottle before she returned. This party would now be the talk of the school. It was worth the twenty bucks they all managed to collect.

Everyone chipped in to make it happen.

When Benny spun the bottle round at Carmela's birthday party, and it landed on her and he secretly went for her breast along with his first kiss; she and he were boyfriend and girlfriend from that moment on. Carmela didn't really have her eyes on Benny, but since he had made her thighs tingle that night, she thought why not! It was at that moment, that they became inseparable. Carmela didn't have a clue what love meant, or what Benny meant. What she did know was when he put his tongue deep in her mouth, and grabbed her breast ever so tight, she would do anything for him. And so she did! It was right then and there that Carmela lost it when they were making out in the balcony of the Strand, and just like that she became pregnant. She almost wasn't sure that it had happened, because before she knew what had happened Benny got up to get popcorn and left her there alone in the dark.

She never thought of herself as an easy girl, she always followed all the rules, she tried her best in school, she helped her mom; yet, somehow there in the dark of the balcony of The Strand her legs flew wide, Benny swooped in, it felt so good, and the movie was over, along with life as she had known it before.

Carmela knew that things had changed, but not quite sure how. She thought her period would return as she counted the days. She wasn't feeling too well in the early morning hours. She tried talking to Benny. He wasn't sure why she wanted to speak to him. He didn't want to listen to Carmela, and he certainly never wanted to tell his parents if it turned out that Carmela was pregnant. In truth, he wouldn't even own up to his indiscretion. He flat out told Carmela that it wasn't possible, that she had a reputation around school with other guys and broke it off then and there. Carmela cried a lot that night and decided to confide in the only person who would understand--- her mother.

Carmen proceeded to yell at Carmela, calling her a whore, and the next week she did what was the only thing she could think of, shipped her off to the home for wayward girls several towns over. The school was notified that Carmela needed to improve her grades, which in truth were very poor, and she was being sent to live with her aunt in Virginia.

Carmen helped Carmela pack her suitcase, drove her to the bus the following week, and shipped her out of town. Somehow this occurrence was normal at Woodlake High, and no one questioned where she was. Benny went about his life.

Now, Carmen never stopped loving her daughter, but when calling Carmela, she didn't ask too many details because it was enough that she had to support Carmela, and the house, and keep all the spinning plates in the air; a new baby was totally out of the question. Her sixteen-year-old wouldn't be raising "it," she would wind up raising "it." The feedings, the long drives in the car at night to get "it" to sleep, the numerous doctor's appointments, the thousands of diaper changes; oh the list could go on and on. She referred to as an "it" when speaking to her daughter, because calling it a baby or grandchild would make it all too impossible to ever deal with, and so she just didn't deal with it. Nine months, she thought, it would all be over, the "It" would be adopted out, her daughter would be home, and life could go back to normal, whatever normal was. Carmen didn't want Carmela to follow in her footsteps. Carmen wanted Carmela to leave this God forsaken town, go to college, travel the world, marry rich; anything but what Carmela's life had been so far. This was just an unfortunate blip in the road, and Carmen wanted Carmela to pick herself up, and move ahead.

"How's your daughter doing, Carmela?" she would often hear in the Woodlake Junior High's hallways. Carmen always managed to say how well Carmela was doing, how she loved her new school, but that maybe she would be coming home after summer vacation. It was now eight months since that moment in The Strand Balcony. Her weekly calls to Carmela, were now almost daily. She refused to go visit. She knew that such a move would make her prone to indecision and that was unacceptable. It seemed she had persuaded Carmela to sign the papers and forfeit motherhood. She'd have many more opportunities in her life.

Nine and half months passed, and Carmen stood at the bus stop to pick up Carmela returning at last. She watched the buses enter the Woodlake Station, and finally Carmela stepped off the bus looking as she did those many months ago. She looked the same Carmen thought, yet she seemed older somehow. Her beautiful, talented daughter could now go forward without any baggage of a caring for someone before she was ready. Carmen knew this was the best decision for her child.

She hugged her daughter, who just stood ridged. Her arms didn't envelope her mother as she always had before, she didn't make eye contact, she merely waited for the bus driver to get down to remove her suitcase from under the bus. "Let's go home Carmela," Carmen happily said. Carmela wanted to get back on the bus, but she had nowhere else to go. Her mother grabbed the suitcase and noticed a pink blanket sticking out of the side. She looked away, and gently led her daughter into her car. "You know school starts again in another two weeks. So glad you're home."

Chapter 10

Mr. Wright's Fall From Grace

September was approaching. The summer had been one of innocence and freedom. Every afternoon when the sun lowered its heavy rays, Toby would jump on her bike and await the insect dusting by Buzz in his truck. His primary job was to make sure the invasive plants did not attack Woodlake's giant pines. Yet, in the summertime, he had the added responsibility of dusting the foliage with chemicals to prevent the spread of insect invasions upon the helpless inhabitants of Woodlake. It was like being inside a tornado from the Wizard of Oz movie. Toby waited as Buzz's truck rounded the corner and she'd follow behind, weaving in and out of the cloudlike smoke-filled debris it left behind.

During the intense hot summer days, WOR, a TV channel which came out of New York, had a program called the Million Dollar Movie. The Million Dollar movie repeated the same movie twice a day for a week. Toby and her friend Linda would lay on her living room floor, listen to the opening theme, which was from Gone With the Wind, eat potato chips, and drink Coca Colas. After watching Yankee Doodle Dandy, starring Jimmy Cagney, twice a day for seven afternoons and evenings, the girls were able to sing the words to every George M. Cohen's patriotic classics. "Give my regards to Broadway, remember me to Harold Square," each would belt out to their imaginary adoring fans.

The summers were stress free. No school, no homework, and no rules. Sometimes to avoid boredom, the sprinkler would be dragged out on the lawn. With bathing suits and water guns, everyone would run back and forth through the gyrating water, cooling off if only for a moment. If Toby and Linda got ambitious, a lemonade stand would be set up. A wooden plank across two boxes and a pitcher was easy to assemble. Ten cents a glass. They would read Little Lulu and Archie comic books and wait for customers. A day of bringing home one dollar meant they could jump on their bikes once more and head to Bob's for a chocolate shake.

Such days of relaxing were drawing to a close, and white shorts and sneakers were getting ready to be put away. It was that unspoken rule of no white after Labor Day. Toby's shoulders started to droop as she awaited her first days again at Woodlake Junior High. She had heard that there was a new teacher joining the staff, Mr. Frederick Wright. It was bad enough having to return to school but having to adjust to a new teacher on top of it all, made it that more discouraging.

After the Labor Day weekend ended, Toby knew it was going to be a very long autumn and winter. As she entered Woodlake Junior High and went into her homeroom, she was faced with Mr. Wright. He had dark glasses, hair that looked like a comb never touched it, and wore a crisp white shirt. His beady eyes penetrated Toby as she handed him the white paper with her schedule attached to it as she sat down rapidly in the desk that he had assigned her. At least she was able to look out the window. Last year she had talked too much, which wasn't out of the ordinary for her, and was moved up front for the remainder of the term. She was determined to learn her lesson and keep her mouth shut.

There was the obligatory Star-Spangled Banner blaring over the intercom, a reading from the bible, usually the Psalms, the welcome back speech from Principal Ribner, and then Mr. Wright approached the class.

"My name is Mr. Frederick Wright. I will be your homeroom teacher for the remainder of the year, as well as your English teacher. I do not want to see anyone tardy for my classes. I expect everyone to listen and follow directions. I do not allow for assignments to be turned in late, and I will be in touch with your parents if anyone disobeys these rules. Any questions?" No one had any questions, and Toby's stomach began to churn. She knew immediately that Mr. Wright was someone she wasn't going to like. As she turned her head to gaze into the street, her stomach let out an extremely loud grumbling sound. Embarrassed, she snapped her head back into the direction of Mr. Wright who was standing directly in front of her desk. "Are you ok Miss Lester?" Toby just stared and shook her head up and down, indicating that all was well. She couldn't believe that this was the first day of class, and he already knew her last name. She was sure that this was going to be a very long year.

Never had Woodlake Junior High seen the likes of Mr. Wright. He was always standing in the doorway of the classroom before any of the students arrived. He didn't care to socialize with the other teachers. This job was all business to him. He had been hired to teach English, and he didn't intend to deviate from that path. No one knew if he was married or not, but they assumed he was because his pants were starched and pressed along with those crisp, starched white long-sleeved shirts and striped ties. He wore a suit jacket to class which he'd draped over the back of his desk chair, and his shoes were always polished. He left little time for small talk with his students.

"Class, let's begin. Open your notebooks. I expect everyone to take notes." At the exact moment the bell, which indicated that class began, stopped ringing, was the exact moment Mr. Wright began his lecture.

"I know you will be interested to learn that our first piece of literature this year will be George Orwell's Animal Farm." As he handed out copies of the book to each student, he continued, "I expect you to read the first five chapters by next week. Make sure you put a brown paper bag protective cover on your copy. I will be testing you on its contents. Today we will be covering…."

As he spoke, most of the classes' eyes began to glaze over with boredom and disinterest. Toby quickly began to focus on Mr. Wright as he positioned himself upon his desk. He leaned on top of it with his legs stretched out in front of him. He kept twisting his legs back and forth on top of each other. Toby began to count how many times they flipped from side to side and was almost put in a trance and awakened when the bell finally rang, and she could leave his room for the day. She pushed her copy of Animal Farm into her book bag and left quickly.

Her next stop was math, a subject she despised. It made no sense to her and usually was confusing and gave her stomach problems. Toby didn't enjoy going to school; she didn't like being confined with rules and regulations, but at eleven she knew she'd have to make the best of it, which was forever a challenge.

Lunch finally arrived and Toby knew that after a few more classes she would be heading home. She hoped that *The Spot* would have Cliff Notes for Animal Farm. After hearing Mr. Wright drone on about its content, she didn't think she'd ever possibly understand any of it.

Upon her arrival at The Spot, it seemed that no copies of Cliff Notes of Animal Farm were anywhere to be found. Cliff Notes summarized and simplified any books of literature that Toby and all her junior high friends desperately needed to slog through the maze that Mr. Wright forced upon them. It was apparent that the rest of her classmates had the exact thoughts as did Toby. This was very painful for her to discover because she knew she would have to read the entire dreaded book. Failing English class was not an option.

The next day, Mr. Wright gave a lecture on the background of Animal Farm. He paced up and down the room and didn't seem to notice half of the students were falling asleep, while others were passing notes back and forth to one another. There was a pool going on by the girls as to who could come closest to picking how many times Mr. Wright would turn and go back and forth to the wall, and another by the boys to count when he was sitting on his desk how many times he would shift his ankles from left to right.

Mr. Wright was so caught up in lecturing from his extensive notes that he rarely looked up, "The struggle for preeminence between Leon Trotsky and Stalin emerges….." Toby didn't have a clue as to what he was saying, nor did she care. She did however enjoy watching him pace the room like a prison guard. She was hoping that she could pass this class, as she frequently prayed for most of her classes. "Dear God, I'm not the best student, but please if you could give me a little help, I promise to be kind to others." Toby silently repeated.

It was almost test day and Toby had managed to struggle through the first five chapters of Animal Farm. "We will have a brief review today," Mr. Wright announced. It was an extremely hot September day, even for New Jersey and Mr. Wright opened all the classroom windows. He got the large hook attached to a long wooden pole to catch onto the shades and up they flew. Uncharacteristically, he rolled up his sleeves. He did something that never happened before, he pulled his wooden desk chair in front of his large wooden desk, sat down, and began rocking back and forth. Pushing off the floor with his right leg as the chair tilted back and the loud banging of the chair leg as it pounded against the hard wood floors below. As the chair teetered and banged onto the floor all eyes got entranced with the rhythmic beats.

The oppressive heat was overwhelming him, and he couldn't bring himself to do his usual pacing. The class somehow snapped to attention because this was not the Mr. Wright they expected. All bets were off, and everyone became fixated on counting how many times the legs of the chair went back and forth knocking against the pine boards. It seemed like a circus act with Mr. Wright balancing on the two front legs of the chair before he continued to speak tipping the chair in the opposite direction.

As Mr. Wright's excitement grew in his explanations, the rocking increased, "Manor Farm symbolizes…." Yada, yada, yada was all that any of the students heard. All eyes focusing on the chair and wondering if Mr. Wright would tilt it again. 45, 46, 47, 48, they began to whisper; awaiting the fiftieth mark. "He's going to reach 100," Billy exclaimed. "Nope I don't think he'll get to 60," Sally blurted out. "He'll get there," Toby responded. Just as he was approaching forty-nine Mr. Wright lost his balance in its backward position and down the chair fell, his head slightly grazing the desk as he tumbled directly down on to the floor.

Laughter echoed through the open windows and doorways, as everyone sprung up out of their desks viewing Mr. Wright supine on the floor, dazed and flustered.

"Sit down, everyone sit down, get back to your seats NOW!" he uncharacteristically yelled to the frenzied mass.

Enraged he jumped to his feet. Between the screaming and laughter, entered Mr. Calvern, vice principal, the arbiter of bad news. With a single piercing glance sweeping across the room, everyone instantly rushed to their desks and folded their hands. Not a sound was heard. Everyone stopped breathing. Mr. Calvern then noticed Mr. Wright's bloody face and escorted him directly to the nurse's office. The next day a substitute appeared and stayed until the following week. Eventually, Mr. Wright returned. He never spoke of the incident. Toby, nor any of the students dared to discuss among themselves what had happened. Some weren't sure if somehow they had been at fault and felt guilty of being so unkind, while others reveled in their inner thoughts that he deserved what had happened. Either way they all kept silent.

Mr. Wright continued to teach but it was a day no one at Woodlake Junior High ever forgot. Before the start of every school year when new students walked into his classroom, they always whispered about his mishap wondering what exactly happened. They were never very clear about it and yet, it was forever remembered as the day Mr. Wright had fallen from grace.

Chapter 11

Curse of the Jersey Devil

School had rapidly begun several weeks ago, summer was a memory, and children were laser focused on Halloween. The annual Halloween window shop painting contest would be underway soon along with the town's costume contest. Labor Day had passed as Woodlake's trees were blazing. Their green leaves morphed into shades of browns, oranges, golds and vibrant reds. The warmer summer air turned to cooler jacket and sweater weather as birds contemplated migrating south.

Children peddled everywhere on bikes. Parks were filled with families strolling along the sidewalks and meandering the pathways of Woodlake's beautiful lake enjoying the blue sky and glorious Jersey pines. On weekends, people drove to the pumpkin farms on the outer perimeter of town to pick out the perfect one to carve and display in front of their homes for all to enjoy.

Lillian had begged Bob to leave the diner in other hands

for a drive out into the country to see the seasonal changes. She knew he was conjoined to his beloved diner. She was proud of his dedication, but this time of the year would soon be over, and she wanted them to enjoy it together before it drifted all too quickly into winter. For some unknown reason, perhaps her wistful smile, he ultimately agreed. He had summoned Rosaline and Ginger to run things for a few hours. Bob set out all the fixings for sandwiches for them to sell and left detailed instructions on how to pour his famous pancake batter mix. He checked and rechecked his long list of what to do and not to do. His Lillian was always at the register when things got busy. She had his dinner warming in the oven whenever he arrived home late, and never asked for much. He knew that today he had to let go and go along on her planned outing.

At precisely noon, she appeared at the entrance, and beckoned Bob to hurry before they missed this opportunity. With mild reluctance, Bob took off his spattered apron, spoke his instructions to Rosaline and Ginger once more, and joined Lillian down the stairs into their big red truck. In the back bay was a huge basket full of sandwiches and homemade cookies, that were Bob's favorites, and a silver thermos with a red plaid screw top lid to hold warm tomato soup. She had thought of everything. She had even managed to clean the old blanket that was draped over the boxes in their garage, so they could lay it on the ground when they stopped for this delicious picnic.

"Lillian, why all this fuss?" As Bob blushed, Lillian was glad that after all their years of marriage, he still acted like this was their first date.

"Don't be silly, I know that getting away today was no easy task for you, and I wanted it to be extra special," she lied a little because if she let Bob know that she was a bit peeved at how she wished this should be a weekly event; but after much cajoling had to be content that this moment was here at last.

She knew from the beginning that prying Bob away from the diner would never be easy. On most days she accepted this, but then came the times when she just couldn't. When Bob's dad fell to the floor and the baton was passed from father to son, even that day Bob couldn't shut the doors of the diner full of customers to mourn. He continued serving everyone until he shut the doors at midnight and wept in her arms. She was so angry then and held it in knowing that Bob's way of dealing was to continue cooking and letting things go on as usual. She was angry when he missed weddings, christenings, and movies at the Strand. She got used to going alone, but she sometimes wondered why things couldn't be different.

Today anyway, she would try and let all those feelings go and enjoy the wonder of the Jersey fall. As she glided into the passenger seat Bob rested his hand on hers and started up the truck.

"Let's get going Lillian. This is your day." "It's our day," Lillian answered.

"Yes, our day. I heard on Route 61 a new pumpkin patch is ready and they sell freshly picked sweet corn and apple cider, and there are places where we could spread out our blanket and have our picnic." Lillian was excited that today she was going to have Bob all to herself.

"Sounds just perfect."

Lillian could see that Bob was trying to make this a special day even though, he kept checking his watch. He was anxious. It was a perfectly normal, busy Saturday afternoon at the diner, and here he was driving to some pumpkin patch Lillian thought that Bob must have been terribly upset. "Do you want to turn back? You seem distracted."

"No, No. I'm sorry. I am very glad to be with you today. Don't worry about me. You know it is just a habit of mine, checking my watch. It's fine."

Lillian sat back in the truck and at last started to look out the window. She realized that if she didn't take in every second it would all disappear, and she'd have no one else to blame but herself. The pines were leading the way and the maples and oaks, who were turning their hues blasted out a magnificent rainbow as the truck sped by. Each bend in the road displayed a variety of trees. The maples had splashes of yellows glowing in the bright sunlight. The oaks were shades of crimson and gold. Stately weeping willows hung their arms and just watched. It was as if a painter had taken out his brushes and in those quiet late hours had worked diligently to cover every last leaf with strokes of colors that led the way.

"Bob this is beyond what I had ever expected. Where to, where to?" Lillian was anxious to know where Bob seemed determined to travel. Several miles ago he had purposefully passed the pumpkin patch that she had suggested. He was never a man of spontaneity, and she was sure he had every detail mapped out, yet he refused to say a word as to where his truck was headed. Perplexed as she hung her head out the window passing the patch, she now inquired, "You know we passed the pumpkin patch several miles ago. It's fine with me, but you know I don't like secrets between us," she tried chiding him into a confession, but Bob kept on driving.

New Jersey glowed and shimmied and Lillian felt so lucky to spend this time with Bob as she was determined to soak in each bend in the road minute by minute. It wasn't that her days in the diner working the register weren't important, nor their time alone late at night having him close by, but today just the two of them traveling the open road was what she had hoped for, for so very long. She knew many years ago that to be married to Bob would be a marriage that she'd have to share with his primary love, the diner. She accepted that she would have many days of solitude at home as he worked long hours and yet when she allowed herself to dream; she saw them both traveling in his truck like this moment. This moment that was beyond her expectations.

As they traversed along Jersey's back roads Bob suddenly yelped out, "Be careful or that Jersey Devil might grab you right out of this truck. You do know that he flies with large wings and there have been sightings of the creature within these Jersey barrens?"

"Bob! Stop!" Lillian wanted to laugh at Bob's teasing but that the creature, which many had claimed to see, actually might be out there among the pines. She was sure of that!

The Jersey Devil had many sightings in these Jersey barrens. The first time for Lillian had been when she was a young girl sitting around the campfire at a girl scout sleep away listening to her scout leader, Mrs. Gray, recounting the tale. Lillian huddled close to the other girls, all bundled up in their sleeping bags. The stars were covered over with clouds, and a mist from the nearby lake wafted over the ground.

"It was over two hundred years ago, in this exact location. Right here where we are in these dark, dense Jersey woods. Over there", the leader pointed as she spoke in rapacious tones. All the girls' heads snapped, in complete synchronization, as they turned to look, "lived a woman with her husband Daniel Leeds. Now Ma Leeds had twelve little children who screamed a lot and made Ma Leeds awfully mad. Every morning when Daniel went off to his almanac business, Ma Leeds would go about the day cleaning and cooking and caring for her twelve bratty kids. They never behaved and she was forever chasing them throughout this thick dark forest. Often," the scout leader emphasized, "one of them would disappear. Poof, gone like that!" snapping her fingers.

"When Daniel returned home, they would search for the kids who got lost in the thicket. This annoyed Ma Leeds. She often would be chasing after one of the Leeds' clan hollering at the top of her voice as they scattered everywhere. One gloomy, foggy night as Ma Leeds was about to have her thirteenth child, it so displeased her for none of her children knew how to behave, and so another one was too much for her to bear. In the quiet dim light, she looked up at the stars and spoke, *"Let this child be the devil himself for I cannot stand another human."* The girls huddled closer together and stared into the crackling campfire as the story continued.

"As Daniel arrived home minutes before the infant was born, it all looked fine, but suddenly before their eyes the tiny baby started to transform into a winged creature with fiery eyes and a pointed tail. It stood up on its hooved feet and with a gallop flew out the cabin window never to be seen again." The girls banded even closer inching together as sounds of breaking branches were heard in the distance.

"Now girls", the leader said in hushed tones, "beware, the Jersey devil might be out there!" Just then the girls swore they heard loud pounding galloping footsteps. With that, Miss Bea, the assistant leader, snuck out quietly from the thicket tip toeing her way towards the scouts who screamed with terrified delight. Lillian turned in the opposite direction and was sure she saw a large, open mouthed ferocious creature fly off into the distance. Everyone began to scream and giggle as they turned their heads back and forth, yet Lillian was positive she had seen a bat like creature brush past her into the forest. "Over there I saw it, please believe me," Lillian begged.

The scout master told the girls to quiet down. Again, at that moment; Bea, who hid again in the thicket, bolted out of the woods once more, flapping her arms; as the young girls laughed and screamed louder, delighting in the fun.

Eventually everyone ate s'mores and happily fell asleep, but not Lillian. She couldn't eat or close her eyes. She knew that at any moment the wind was bringing the Jersey devil's flying body back to carry her off.

Her second encounter, Lillian was a teenager and when circling the lake with Mark who bent over to experience his first kiss, but instead received a loud blood curdling scream from Lillian. There up in the tree she believed was the monster flapping its wings and swinging its long, pointed tale. Mark thought he had done something terribly wrong, but when Lillian tried explaining he turned and left, leaving Lillian. She ran home at full speed, never looking back.

Bob's teasing hit her directly on her Achilles' heel. Lillian wanted this to be their special day, but her old fears still lurked in her head. Bob noticed that Lillian wasn't smiling, and he tried changing the subject.

"Lillian, don't worry I will protect you. Remember this is our day." Lillian didn't respond; her heart was beating too fast. She just wanted them to turn around and head back to the diner. How silly she felt having these childish thoughts, but somehow those old fears refused to leave.

Every Halloween people from Woodlake would dress up as the Jersey Devil. There were hundreds of manifestations. Hoofed toes, black capes, pointed tails, and hands with sharp-like pointed fingernails. One of the townships close by even called their hockey team the Jersey Devils. Lillian always flinched a little when her friends, dressed as the winged creature, passed her by during trick or treating. She shook off the children in witch costumes, or the ones wearing white sheets over their heads with holes for eyes as ghosts, but when they dressed up as that monstrous Jersey Devil, she never failed to shudder. It was an irrational reaction that she was very much aware of, but it didn't change a thing.

"Let's head back, the diner probably is packed with people and I am sure they could use our help. We can do this some other time."

All her expectations for this day were quickly fading. She wanted to be back home to a place where she felt safe.

"Two more minutes, then we can turn back. Just two more minutes," Bob lied. The red truck inched further into the woody area.

Lillian almost begging now, "Please Bob I'm not feeling well. It will be getting dark in a few hours and it will be treacherous out here." No matter how she cajoled Bob, he wouldn't listen and kept driving deeper into the woods. At each twist in the road Lillian began clutching the seat and inching nearer to Bob. As the truck made a quick turn, on the edge of the gravel roadway a sign appeared that read, *River's Edge Inn*. Bob quickly steered along the narrow roadway lined with magnificent oak trees and a white picket fence. Magically, an elderly woman wearing a blue flowered apron appeared on the porch of an old quaint inn that backed onto a glistening river setting waving them onto to a small, pebbled pathway that led to the front.

"Over here, just park anywhere. I was expecting you an hour ago, glad you both made it," she said.

There, awash in pink and yellow gingerbread cutouts with a bright red rooster weathervane spinning on the roof, was the most magical bungalow that Lillian had ever seen. Tulips of every color led up to the porch.

Surprised, Lillian looked at Bob, "Why you planned this all along. You never said a word. What shall I do with the lunch I prepared?"

"It will keep," said Bob, "Mrs. Bea has a special lunch all set for us. She told me over the phone that she promised us a private spot in a gazebo out back right next to the river. I want this to be your special day. I know you feel like leaving and heading home, but I knew you wouldn't mind this detour?"

"Bob, I don't know what to say. It's a fairy tale come true." "I love you Lillian, I do."

With that, Bob grabbed Lillian's hand, "Mrs. Bea told me she would be making jelly tarts. Heart shaped, I think. I'm so hungry." Bob bent over and kissed Lillian.

Mrs. Bea began shouting from the porch, "Ok you love birds, lunch is served." Lillian was determined that today was going to be her day. She scanned the forest and thought for a moment that she saw something flying off into the distance, but for now that winged creature and Lillian's fear of the Jersey devil would just have to wait.

"Ok, we're coming."

Chapter 12

The Woodlake Halloween Contest

Nearing the end of October, images of witches and disjointed black cats popped up adorning the mundane shop windows. Most days as people strolled by, they usually viewed ordinary blue checkered dresses draped shabbily on mannequins, red metal toolboxes, or polished brown work boots. Overnight, Casper like ghosts heralding large "BOO!" letters, creepy black bats and eerie goblins of garish green with bulging eyes and pointy ears embellished the shop fronts. Skeletons swung from store ceilings, pumpkins to be sold were stacked high, and dark looming creatures made the children await the night of fantasy and trick or treating to come in the week that followed. To children and adults alike, it seemed as if mysterious beings suddenly appeared to paint these scary and haunting scenes. Maybe the infamous Jersey Devil had once more made his mark.

In reality, it was Woodlake's tradition to have artists

and would-be artists adorn shop windows with fall, and Halloween murals. Anyone willing to risk their artistic ambitions could volunteer to make these fantastical images. The aspiring artists could vie for ribbons of blue, red and white. In addition to the wonderous window decorating, Woodlake had signs announcing the Annual Halloween Costume Contest to be held the night before Halloween in the high school's auditorium.

First prize for the most original costume would be a $10 dollar shopping spree at Woodlake's Five and Ten, as well as $10 for burgers of their choice at Bob's Diner. Woodlake's children were abuzz with plans for this event, and everyone was to attend. Last year's winner was a giant hamburger complete with ketchup, pickles and lettuce made of cardboard and green and red crepe paper. It looked so real that several kids tried biting into it. Little Joey, the winner, was not too upset because he relished the attention.

This was no ordinary costume contest-- witches and ghosts were fine for the door-to-door trick or treating but not for this event. The competition was fierce, and plans were put in place months before. Parents kept their designs very secretive so as not to get stolen. Children were bursting with excitement and found it hard to not let anyone know what this year's costume choices would be.

Bob had decorated every inch of the diner with owls, trolls, and flying monsters that were attached to every booth and upon the walls. It was always a time for the community to ban together to make this a festive, fun event. The Strand theater ran Frankenstein and the Mummy every evening and twice on weekends. Candy was bought by the bagful and at school it was almost impossible to contain the children until Halloween was over. They usually ate way too much candy, but that was the joy of Halloween.

Estelle Pervus had decided to make her daughter the most wonderful mermaid costume one had ever seen. Her own mother never had the time because she had to help out with the family when she was little. Estelle Pervus was a stay-at-home mom, this would be her way of finally bringing home the win she herself had longed for.

She had been sewing sequins on every inch of it, from top to fin, throughout the summer in complete secrecy. In shades of blue, and turquoise, it glistened. There was no way this wouldn't be the number one winner in all of Woodlake. She even constructed a water scene on top of a red radio flyer wagon that her little girl Emily could sit upon and be wheeled onto the stage. There was dark organza seaweed, and jelly fish dangling down the sides cut out of paper and covered in gold glitter. Estelle Pervus wouldn't be side swiped by another cardboard hamburger or packing box television set like Carl's son won with two years ago. This was her moment.

The judges were chosen so as not to have any bias, and they never smiled or addressed any of the contestants. This was serious business for Woodlake and all its entries. These competitions were extraordinary moments in an otherwise quiet and often repetitive day to day existence. Townsfolk needed such moments to spark their imaginations and to have those days to look forward to.

Usually about fifty children paraded across the stage and the auditorium was always packed with parents, grandparents, teachers, and children. Although those children wearing store bought costumes could march across the stage, they had no chance of winning so most chose to participate by cheering and applauding in their seats as each contestant strutted across the stage. After the grand prize was awarded, everyone was treated to candy and punch.

The evening of the contest arrived, and Mr. Waverly

principal of Woodlake High, quieted the audience as best he could. "Let's all rise for the pledge of allegiance and the singing of the Star-Spangled Banner. Now, children we must all behave like proper ladies and gentlemen." Very few listened; babies were fidgeting, toddlers were running around, teenagers were talking to their friends, and parents readied their Brownie cameras as the march of the contestants began.

The judges took out their clip boards, had pencils sharpened and were ready to start calculating each participant. All the judges were somberly taking this event in earnest with their backs to the crowd. There were points for originality, presentation, beauty, funniest, and over all theme. "Look at those sequins!" they'd whisper to each other or "that is amazing!" as the children strutted across the stage. Their clip boards were pressed to their chests. No one dared cheat or share their findings until the final calculations were tallied.

First on stage was a silver painted ladder pushed onto the stage by her dad, where a tiny angel was perched. Six-year-old Wanda was adorable with her white wings covered in cotton and a golden halo made from twisted pipe cleaners. "Smile baby!" her mother loudly whispered backstage, peeking through the curtains, "Let's see that big beautiful smile," but Wanda refused. She almost fell off the ladder as she twisted her body searching for her mommy.

There was a string of cowboys --one with his large golden retriever Biff wearing a makeshift saddle-- ballerinas, and a teenager covered with twigs wearing a green leotard appearing to be a Jersey pine tree. There was a circus clown twirling a red hula hoop got applause from the crowd, several monsters, one with blood oozing from his face which got some titters from the kids watching below, and then Estelle Pervus wheeled out Emily.

As Emily appeared on stage, a wave of applause could

be heard in the auditorium. The glitter from her costume caught the reflections from the overhead spotlights on the stage, and bounced rainbow colors onto the walls. "That's my granddaughter!" could be heard. "Turn here," Emily's dad shouted pointing his Brownie camera her way. Estelle Pervus had coached little Emily who waved graciously to the patrons, blowing kisses everywhere. Emily was nervous and scared but kept smiling for she knew this meant so much to her mom. With the delight coming from the audience, it seemed her win was all sewn up.

By sheer coincidence, and beyond anyone's imagination, next up was Joan Huett's daughter Veronica, lying in a converted baby's crib with a sparkling sign that cleverly read, "Rocked in the Cradle of the Deep," was also dressed as a mermaid. Her costume was also encrusted with sequins. She too had a magnificent costume, as well as fins that Veronica was able to flap back and forth as the crib was placed onto the stage.

A silent gasp could be felt from the crowd. How was this possible? Could it really be happening? Estelle Pervus was devastated and shocked. "This can't be!" she blurted out. Joan Huett could not believe this was happening either. And yet here they were -- both girls almost identical. Never before had anyone dressed their daughters as mermaids and yet to everyone's dismay it had happened!

The judges started scrambling as to what to do, huddling like a group of football players on the edge of the stage. This had never happened before. Not ever!! "We can't give those two girls points for originality, can we? They were dressed almost the same. Both costumes were so clever and beautiful. No, it just wouldn't be fair!" adding and recounting the numbers and crossing out points. They paced back and forth. And so to the horror and overwhelming disappointment of many, they all agreed, the only thing honorable was to give the winning prize to Wanda the angel.

Everyone eventually realized this was the right thing to do, and without a word little Wanda walked away with first prize, still not looking at the crowd. Immediately, lots of people began congratulating Wanda as well as those who had not won and, of course, all contestants receiving beautiful participation certificates.

Estelle Pervus holding back tears, grabbed Emily --who so wanted to stay-- signaled to her husband and the rest of her family, as she stomped home without a word to anyone.

On the other hand, Joan and her daughter Veronica were happy to have participated and ate and drank the punch. "Veronica we sure had fun tonight," she said, hugging her daughter tightly. "I loved it, and can we do it again next year?" Veronica giggled.

Halloween in Woodlake went on as usual the following night. In homes all around town doorbells were ringing, and kids were rushing up walkways asking for candy as they were screaming out, "Trick or Treat!" Doorways flew open as children's pillow sacks and paper bags were stuffed with Nicco wavers, Hershey or Babe Ruth candy bars, handfuls of candy corn; along with candied apples wrapped in bright cellophane wrappers. Sometimes even pennies were sprinkled into the delight of the children.

Yes, indeed it was that magical time of year in Woodlake that no one could ever forget- especially Estelle Pervus, who was sure of a win that never did happen.

Chapter 13

Bob's Dilemma

He grew up watching his dad preparing eggs and flipping pancakes. He watched his dad peppering the hash browns and firing up the oven. While his brothers couldn't wait to attend college and leave Woodlake, he stayed behind to be in the one place that brought him peace, the diner. He couldn't even complete his high school senior year for he knew in his heart of hearts that he would never need that diploma. It was his destiny to be the successor and proprietor of Bob's Diner. No one in Woodlake noticed the seamless transition when Bob senior was gone, and Bob Junior took over. It was magical. It was the order of things. The way it was supposed to be.

Bob's Diner stood there in its' corner of the world. When one rounded the bend, entering Woodlake, and saw the garish neon pink Bob's Diner sign flashing on and off, they knew they were home. Day or night Bob would be peering out from the kitchen and ringing his bell to alert Rosaline that the foods were ready to go. When things got slow, he would amble out front to talk with Rosaline. On special days, his beloved Lilly would come and help up front to work the register, and seat customers. Life was simple and good.

Of course, some days were better than others. There was the death of Bob senior, Bob's rock. It was a day unlike any other, the grill was going, the pancake batter was ready, the coffee permeated the air and in mid-sentence, "Hey, Bob could you….." Bob senior fell to the floor and was no more. At that instant Bob knew what he must do, call the volunteer rescue squad, make funeral arrangements, and keep the diner going. He had no time to mourn or let the people of Woodlake down, this was now his responsibility, and he took it seriously.

There was also the time when his dear Lilly thought she was carrying their child and wasn't. He felt so powerless. He kept telling Lilly that it didn't matter, but she wouldn't listen. She retreated into their home for many days and now seemed somewhat content.

Bob felt serene in his world with his routine of waking up early, walking to work in the dark of the mornings, opening the back door of the diner, and beginning his day. His childhood sweetheart was unwavering in her love for him, and he returned her love without flinching. Few were lucky to lead such a calm, unfettered life and Bob was such a man.

When there were disputes in Woodlake, Bob unflinchingly remained neutral. He did not take sides. He was the man of the people. All people!

Uncharacteristically, on one such innocuous day, Charley Fishburn was running for Mayor, when a verbal fight broke out around the counter.

"Hey, Bob, Charley ain't got a chance in hell of winning. All he ever talks about is fixing up the baseball field. What about the pathways around Woodlake's lake? That baseball field is just fine the way it is. Don't you agree, Bob? You listening, Bob? If our lake had prettier pathways with more flowers, more tourists would come into town. Isn't that true, Bob?"

"So, I hear the front page of the Gazette this week is featuring the updates on the skating rink," responded Bob. "The girl scouts have begun their annual cookie sale. Why just yesterday my Lilly purchased ten boxes of thin mints in front of The Spot. Can you imagine that! She's willing to share them. Any takers?"

George Waller, also running for mayor and a regular at Bob's, chimed in, "I agree those pathways surrounding the lake have gone into complete disarray. Why just last week Toby Lester almost broke her arm when her bike tire got caught in the cracked concrete and she crashed into a tree. The baseball field is fine just the way it's always been, right Bob?" Back and forth the bickering continued week after week. "The baseball practice was delayed last night. Too many puddles where the grass used to be," Charley blustered. "I can't walk around the lake, I'm afraid of falling," George muttered.

If he agreed or not, Bob wasn't going to tell. He just grinned or nodded, that way no one could suspect Bob of throwing his support in either direction. He preferred to stay on the side lines, at least that was his plan.

Things went on this way for months, but as life sometimes does, Bob was thrown an unexpected curve ball. The morning started like any other until Tilly Jones stepped into the diner at 9:15 AM and for some unknown reason lingered there. As she was perusing the pictures and flyers hanging on the diner's cluttered walls, she spotted a rectangular, brown plaque encrusted with a gold trim and gasped as she held tightly to her chest. "Bob, what's this I see," She heralded, and screeched as all heads turned in her direction. "You are a Charley Fishburn supporter! You must want that baseball field refurbished, really bad? A Charley Fishburn supporter in our mist. Why I never!"

Alas, something very small had slipped his mind. Hanging up front by the grand double doors was that nondescript gold-plated plaque that Bob was awarded for his yearly sponsorship of the Woodlake Little League Baseball Team along with many others that Bob had generously donated money. He didn't see the little league as more important than all the others he had given a contribution. There was the award from the Girl Scouts of Woodlake and the Boy Scouts. The Police Benevolent Society, The Library Society, and many other awards for his unwavering support of all community activities. He hadn't thought too much about how this might put him in the middle of Charley and George's run for Mayor. Something so innocent and mundane became the bone of contention as customers took sides.

Bob wanted to explain that he loved the kids; it had nothing to do with who he'd prefer for Mayor, but before he could get the words out, the line was drawn in the sand. From that moment on, the Charley supporters sat at the tables to the right of the kitchen, and George Waller's people on its left. Bob avoided taking sides for weeks and yet he was thrust in the middle.

Bob was at a loss. Always looking forward to his early morning crowd, he now cringed when entering his beloved diner. George's team when ordering would speak only to Rosaline. They couldn't go elsewhere for their usual breakfast or coffee. Although annoyed with Bob, the diner was the only place to be. Charley's crew would glare at their opponents' when stepping inside, and George's group did the same.

Lilly never had to push or cajole Bob to leave the house, and now she found herself acting like a sergeant at arms getting him out the door every morning.

"You're not even dressed. What's going on?"

"I can't take this much longer, Lilly. You'd think I'd been the cause of World War III. I just want things to go back to how they were." As the weeks dragged on Bob was growing sadder and sadder. Everyone began to notice that when they looked into the kitchen his elbows were not leaning on the counter, and his smiling face no longer scanned the room. When people entered the diner, Lilly forgot to greet them, and she seemed lost in thought. This was not good. Not good for Woodlake, not good for Bob's customers, not good for anyone.

So, as it began, it was to end. Two weeks before the election the Woodlake baseball field was miraculously transformed. Where once stood the straggly score board, handwritten with chalk, an electronic one suddenly dominated it with flashing lights. The sagging, broken bleachers were quickly repaired, painted bright blue, and nearby a sparkling concession booth was erected. The field's brown grass turned green overnight. As if that wasn't enough, the pathways around Woodlake's glistening lake were finely cemented. There were no more cracks or jagged crumbling walkways. Tulips of red, yellow, and pink graced their every twist and turn. A new wooden arbor heralded people to the walkways ahead. Welcome To Woodlake, the Happiest Place in the World, it read. Hundreds of birds, American robins, blue jays, even Red Winged Blackbirds, returned to flock there along with many walkers admiring the beauty.

Everything magically was in order. Who was responsible, people speculated. The question went unanswered. The town folks weren't sure what had taken place and yet, there was a change in the air. When walking in the dark to open the diner, as he had for years, Bob started smiling again. He completed making the coffee and turned on the lights. Bob stuck his head out of the kitchen, "Morning ladies, hi guys," briefly welcoming, watching intently as the early customers arrived. Everyone mingling again, "Morning Bob! How's Lilly?" The election eventually took place. No one seemed to care who won, especially not Bob.

Chapter 14

A Day Like No Other

Study hall was no place to study, and it wasn't in a hall of any shape or size. Study hall was a self-contained portion of the school, inside the cafeteria, before or after lunch. Study hall was supposed to get adolescents to focus, concentrate and get their work done. Toby had no intention to study nor get any of her work done. She'd so much prefer being straddled over her bed, legs dangling over its side, piles of records stacked on her record player blaring out the hits of the day. She would seriously attempt to study, but it rarely happened.

Anyplace would be better than to be stuck in Woodlake Junior High's obligatory study hall, ruminated Toby. As a girl of twelve, she had no input in such decision making, and so here she would stay fighting with herself to be quiet and pretend to be reading.

She had at least several chapters to review for her history class, math problems to complete and a report to finish for her geography teacher. There were less than 30 days to go until Christmas break, and every day that she crossed off the calendar made time go by a little quicker.

Just yesterday, she had walked to the Woodlake Library and taken out several books on Belgium. Miss Farber had assigned countries to every student and Toby picked Belgium because of its size. "Class", Miss Farber reiterated, "The United States is over 300 times the size of Belgium." She thought because it was very small the report wouldn't have to be too long. She later found out that no matter the country's size, everyone had to write a six-page report with a map of the country, its flag, and with interesting facts. There were very few books at Woodlake's small Library, so Toby had to stay and copy lots of information out of the large red World Book Encyclopedia. The librarian, Miss Hodges, was very kind yet stern as she handed the large B volume to Toby.

"Please handle it carefully and return it to me when you are finished. No mussy fingers please or candy anywhere near that volume!" She lectured to Toby. Toby had heard that abomination before and sauntered over to the nearest library table. Toby scribbled facts about Belgium's language, population and its capital, Brussels. The pictures of beautiful lace intrigued her; but with Miss Hodges glancing at Toby every ten minutes, she was hurrying things along to leave and be done with it all. She kept trying to write faster. She imagined that at any moment, Miss Hodges would storm over and snatch the book away from her. Although that never happened, it gave Toby an excuse to leave earlier than planned and escape the constant vigilance of Miss Hodges.

It would only be another thirty minutes to class. Lunch time was held in the same school cafeteria, and although most kids didn't like the food served there, Toby found it exotic. The sliced peaches, fried chicken and mashed potatoes were her favorites. For a mere twenty-five cents even a small carton of milk was included along with a chocolate chip cookie. She'd usually eat with a few friends and talk about boys.

Today was Friday and soon after Toby would walk home for a weekend of complete fun and freedom. Since the library was closed on Sundays, she still would have to spend another few hours there tomorrow morning finishing up her report. Yet, aside from completing her class work, there would be enough hours left to go outside and possibly ride her bike and forget school for the remainder of the weekend.

Dismissal wasn't coming fast enough. Toby tried working on her math problems, but watching the clock was more engaging. She would always attempt to tell herself that any work completed in study hall would free up her weekend, but somehow that trick didn't work. Today she slipped a teen magazine inside her history book and learned how to easily shuffle it back out of sight when the teacher in charge walked past her table. As she noticed hand of the clock going past 1:30, it was now 1:35, she began to wonder why the bell hadn't rung letting everyone get up and proceed to their next class.

Toby had already shoved everything into her briefcase, and was ready to stand up when Mr. Ribner, the principal, came on the address system, "Students and faculty it is with a heavy heart that I must announce our dear, beloved President Kennedy has been shot."

Toby wasn't sure what she heard. She turned to look at the teacher in charge and the other students and no one was saying a word. There was absolute silence. No one spoke or moved. Everyone remained frozen. Toby thought immediately that President Kennedy would be fine, but her next thought was—what if he wasn't? Her heart raced. She wanted to leave and go home. She wanted to be safe.

She was no longer thinking about weekend plans. Those thoughts vanished from her head. Her thoughts of school and reports also left as fear creeped into her mind. "Was there an attack on our country? Who would be next? They might be killing everyone?" Toby shook. Just last week she had seen pictures of Caroline and John, the young children of the President and his wife playing on the White House lawn in the recent Life Magazine that was delivered every week to her house. She always looked forward to lying on the living room floor on top the orange shag carpet and thumbing through its glossy photos.

Again, the silent room heard a second announcement from Principal Ribner in his stern and strident voice, "We would like everyone to proceed to their lockers NOW, get your belongings in an orderly fashion, and leave campus immediately!"

Again, Toby couldn't believe what she had just heard. Under normal circumstances leaving school early would be fantastic, but not today and not like this. Still in complete silence, students like robots rapidly turned, exiting the large cafeteria. There were a few whispers to one another to make sure what they had heard on the loudspeaker was true. Toby hoped that her mother was home. She went to her locker, mindlessly got the books she needed, and left Woodlake Junior High along with everyone else.

No sooner had she walked two blocks from the school when her father pulled alongside her in his pink Plymouth, "Hop in kid." She couldn't hold it in anymore and tears rushed down her face. Toby slid into the large bench seat and pushed up against her father. She squeezed him tight. "Is he going to be ok? President Kennedy, is he going to be ok?" she pleaded.

"No, I'm afraid he isn't."

Toby looked at her father and knew that this was a day like no other. She leaned even closer to her father and leaned her head on his shoulder. The huge engine started to roar. The world for Toby and the people of Woodlake had changed just then.

Camelot was over.

Toby and her dad both drove home in silence.

Chapter 15

The Date

Nathan Twitters slowly walked up to Bob's Diner for his first date ever. High school, college and twenty years of work, and yet never a date. His years alone were lived one day at a time. He had few relationships with others. His mother forever. He never knew his father. He learned to put one foot in front of the other and move ahead in life—to no particular place with no particular goal. His dreams of leaving Woodlake and finding more in the city never came to pass. He reluctantly returned to Woodlake. A return to a life of sameness. Get up, shower, eat, go to work, come home, eat, watch TV, go to sleep and repeat it again and again. Every single day. Nathan didn't question his life until he ate one too many dinners with his mother every Sunday.

"Nathan, I went to Bob's Diner the other day, and do you know they painted the entrance pink? Can you imagine such a thing? I mean one would think that Bob might have asked if his customers approved of that. I always thought that the red looked fine the way it was."

Nathan never added to the conversation because his mother spoke of things of little relevance to Mr. Twitters. She spoke of things of little relevance to anyone. The pictures he produced inside his head were more interesting than his mother's words. He just nodded and kept quiet. He was high in the Alps, another time walking along the Great Wall of China, and even in the Outback of Australia photographing hopping kangaroos. Unable to make a life in New York City, but an hour and half from Woodlake, he traveled within his thoughts.

When he was eight years old, his mother had signed his permission slip to go to visit the Museum of History in New York City. The night before he was to go, he came down with the measles and never got there. When he briefly lived in the city, he was so consumed with finding a job that there was never any time for exploring. He stored his dreams away.

A corner of Nathan's apartment was stacked high with travel books. His National Geographic's monthly subscription was his doorway to the world. Nathan Twitters tried to make the best of his simple existence. He didn't know that today all of that might change. Yet, he knew that this day was no ordinary day.

There was something about Rosaline that made him decide to connect. He didn't dwell on what that connection was. To go there would be to travel into unknown territory. He understood that it was not going to be easy nor comfortable. Rosaline reached out to him. She had ventured into his protected space of vulnerability. Was it going to be enough to connect with someone who wasn't his mother? He wasn't sure what was ahead in this journey; but he knew he must travel there. He instinctively knew if he didn't move forward, he might never get another chance.

He scanned the empty walls of his apartment. Only a

calendar hung next to the refrigerator in his small galley kitchen. In bright red crayon was circled today for his meeting with Rosaline. He went to his closet and changed from one white shirt to another white shirt. He put on his newly purchased blue tie, and his familiar red jacket.

As Mr. Nathan Twitters turned to lock his apartment door, he felt a newness to the same repetitive twist of the key. He counted each step as he walked the three floors down, and the five blocks to Bob's diner. Each step felt different as if he had never traveled this way before. He didn't turn back to his apartment as he had done in the past. He strode up to the landing at Bob's Diner with determination. He pushed open the double doors and there standing in front of him was Rosaline. All he could see was her face and her smile. He didn't notice how her legs trembled nor her bright freshly polished waitress shoes.

"I am glad to see you, Rosaline."

"I am glad to see you, Nathan."

Nathan nodded as he opened the double doors and let Rosaline pass in front of him. He followed behind her and looked at her hair as they approached the sidewalk. She always had it bunched up on top her head. Now it tumbled down to her shoulders. As she slowly walked, he noticed the shadows of her silhouette dancing onto the sidewalk under their feet and he smiled. It wasn't like other times he walked this way. He usually walked with a purpose to go to work or to a store, but now he listened to the birds. He had never noticed evening bird songs, but with Rosaline his senses were inching open.

He hadn't planned where they would go, or what they would do. Rosaline didn't know where they would go or what they would do. She didn't care. Nathan then heard words come out of his mouth. Words that he remembered from hundreds of movies he had watched alone, "Wanna go see a new movie tonight at the Strand?" He kept on walking as Rosaline followed.

Three blocks of quiet. They arrived at the Strand. Nathan asked the young girl chewing gum at the ticket window for two tickets. Nathan had never bought two tickets. Rosaline had never sat with anyone but herself at the Strand. It was good and fine. Again, Nathan did what he had seen in many movies and bought a large popcorn and two Cokes. It was good and it was fine.

No one in the dark movie theater could have imagined that Nathan and Rosaline had climbed the Himalayas, but they had. They barely watched the movie. They found it almost impossible. Once, Rosaline grabbed for the popcorn and her arm grazed Nathan's hand. At another time Nathan's elbow brushed against Rosaline's as he sat quietly, often catching a sideward glance of Rosaline by his side.

As the movie ended, and the credits rolled across the screen, the lights came on; both Rosaline and Nathan sat until every popcorn kernel was finished. Nathan and Rosaline eventually stood up. Neither wanted to go. Neither wanted it over.

Nathan finally speaking, "I suppose it's late, I'll walk you home." Rosaline nodded yes. Nathan followed quietly, letting Rosaline guide him to a place he had never been, nor knew about. The Jersey fireflies lit the way as they approached her tiny gingerbread like house. Nathan followed her to the door and stood slightly back watching her turn the key.

"Thank you Nathan this was the best day…." Before she ended her sentence Nathan leaned in and kissed her quickly. Right then. Right there. Somewhat embarrassed, he turned to walk down the pathway but not before uttering, loud enough for Rosaline to hear, "My best day too!"

Chapter 16

The Girls

Bob's Diner was that place to go and escape if one wanted, or the place to rush in for a quick bite. Day or night, it stood in Woodlake as a monument to consistency where a burger was a burger, and a shake was a shake. Everyone knew what to expect and everyone liked it that way.

In Woodlake, life moved at different paces for different people. The kids attending junior high were always in a frenetic rush when entering Bob's, "Two shakes, one chocolate, one vanilla, whip cream on both. Hi. Bye," and out the door they went rushing to a baseball game, the library, or to play in the park. No time for conversation with Rosaline or Bob, just in and off to wherever.

The high school kids loved to stop by after school and sit crammed in a booth, playing music on the juke box and drink ice cream sodas. They always had mountains of fries with gobs of ketchup, not wanting to finish their homework just yet, but instead catch up with friends before completing book reports and algebra that took hours of concentration. They happily sat and were glad to be left alone.

The regulars, who had retired years ago, loved drinking cups and cups of coffee, listening to the tales of the day, and swapping gossip of the town. Sometimes, moms would stop in for a brief reprieve from hauling children from activity to activity, and dads to decompress from the daily grind of life. Bob's Diner was not just a stop to eat, but a sanctuary from the hustle of life.

Rosaline had her regulars at Bob's diner, and "The Girls" were the women that came every Friday evening at precisely 5:30. They hadn't been girls for a very long time, but you could always find them sitting in the booth closest to the bathrooms, laughing and sitting for hours over sodas, hot teas, and occasionally apple pie with vanilla ice cream on the weeks when they were off their diets. Being off their diets was a frequent occurrence, but Rosaline would always politely ask, "Hey ladies, want that dessert menu tonight?"

"Got any more of the blueberry pie, or apple pie?" or "Oh, no Rosaline can't you see we are watching our weight?" It was never apparent to Rosaline, but they felt after losing five pounds everyone should have noticed.

Mary was always in her black slacks and long-sleeved blouse, worn to hide her brown age marks up and down her arms, which after seventy years, no one noticed but Mary. "Hey, Roz did that young man ever come back to take you to dinner?" Mary prodded. Rosaline blushed. Secrets lasted seconds in Woodlake.

Irene, spreading around the middle, with her red pedal pushers and beaded blouse chimed in, "We hear he is a fine teacher and doesn't talk much, but once you snag him, he'll open up." Irene squeezed into the booth and immediately started to scrutinize the menu which always seemed odd because she could have recited it by heart with all her hundreds of visits throughout the decades.

Shirley, around 70 as well and tastefully dressed in a matching beige polyester pants suit, was seeing that Rosaline was beginning to become uncomfortable with the interrogation.

"Hey ladies, enough. Roz has work to do, tell her your order so she can get back to the kitchen. I'm sure she has other people to tend to," Shirley demanded.

Late in the afternoon, every week the "Girls" would attend a free lecture at the Y and when it was done, they'd head over to Bob's. There had always been the four of them.

It had been four of them for over thirty years, but recently a single phone call changed all that. One of them decided that these women were merely acquaintances, never friends and left the tight knit group with a terse phone call to say just almost those exact words, "I have decided after much thought, you were merely acquaintances. Never friends, and never were anything more than that! If I happen to see you somewhere, I will say hello." Bang went the receiver as she hung up.

It came out of the blue, like a violent stroke that ravishes the body leaving one helpless. It's how things sometimes happened in Woodlake.

The "Girls" had for years done everything as a unit and found out that this moving wagon wasn't going to be running as they expected. When the phone was placed down on its receiver their bond was over, and yet the memories lingered. The fourth cog of the wagon had come off and somehow the "Girls,", unbalanced now, had to adjust and adapt and move forward.

At first it didn't seem real. "She'll call soon. It was just a lapse of the moment. She didn't really mean anything," Shirley spoke. But, she never called again, nor inquired about her friends, and they did the same. "After all she had initiated the decision, and she must live with it", Mary added.

There was never an event, a Friday at Bob's that all four wouldn't be seen together. "One for all and all for one!" they'd often chant like the Musketeers. Yet, in a single, startling moment the four became the three. Here the "Girls" sat week after week chatting about life, the daily goings on, whatever came into their heads. They refused to relinquish the consistency of it all. In a single, startling moment the four instantly morphed into the three. Yet, here the "Girls," continued to sit every week and continued to chat about the daily goings on, whatever flashed into their heads. The refused to relinquish the consistency of it all. They couldn't allow things to be changed or worse; lost forever.

As difficult a change as this was, especially for the three dear friends left behind, they understood going forward was how it would be from than on. They all knew someone was missing; but had learned in life that there were unforeseen things that happened. There were good things; but this unfortunately was not one of those.

There was Mary- very American, she even referred to herself as the W.A.S.P. She was a member of the garden club, who attended church every Sunday, and ate ham on white bread with mayonnaise. Mary had lost her husband several years ago, and forever after was looking for someone to fill the void, but up to now, hadn't. Irene and Shirley's husbands were usually in the mix, but never at these Fridays at Bob's. The "Girls" led their own lives during the week, but somehow the weekly meet up brought them close. They needed to connect, to gossip and join one another.

Irene was the only one of the group to have a child, and

Mary and Shirley liked to hear what Irene's son was up to. He had finally moved out into his own apartment and was teaching in the next township over. They doted on his every escapade and lavished him with gifts on every occasion.

Shirley's six cats were her babies, and she rarely left Woodlake for fear that they wouldn't be properly taken care of. The "Girls" immediate small families made them grow very close and become the larger family they always yearned for.

Thanksgiving, Easter, Christmas, Birthdays, Anniversaries and Passover Seders they sat at one another's tables. Funerals were sadly part of their life transitions, too. When Mary lost Wen they gathered round to ease her pain, and during every hospitalization of Irene's cancer treatments they were close by or on the phone.

It was their connection and intertwining of stories and gossip. Their constant weight issues, shopping, and aging. When the four became three that was a difficult and unforeseen transition. They had watched the one who was no longer named do the same to others in the past, but somehow, they never saw it coming. They had listened to her tell them stories over the years about ending friendships with family members, with other friends; yet it would never be us, they believed. "I just decided that Sharon was too overbearing. She never let me speak and so I am not going to talk to her again," she'd glibly say. It seemed like an angry kid on the playground picking themselves up and walking away. Not an adult woman.

That bond that they deeply shared was gone in a moment. Not unlike a death. Alive but not. Here but gone. The bane of her leaving was it never was explained to the "Girls." They also knew if it was explained it still would remain a mystery for how could such a bond be over forever .

The "Girls" belonged to one another. They cared for one another. The four were no more four, but three. The nameless one remained in their thoughts. Too painful to even utter her name; but tonight at Bob's they were able to just be.

The "Girls" chose to live life and go forward. In their quiet, alone times they would remember the missing fourth, but for now it was the three. All was good, laughter flowed, and time continued to move ahead.

Chapter 17

Guiding Light

Temporarily relieved of his teaching duties for the day, Nathan Twitters was assigned to monitoring the halls today at Woodlake's Elementary School. He directed and watched the children lining up to receive the Salk sugar cubes to prevent Polio. After the pledge of allegiance and the Lord's Prayer, Mrs. Brown, the third-grade teacher, announced that all her students were to line up in single file and go to the auditorium.

Nathan had heard about the terrible polio outbreak many times on the six o'clock evening news, and he certainly didn't want to be subjected to the virus in any form. Black and white photos of children and adults stuck inside monstrous iron lung machines for months and possibly years, were on the front of every newspaper, and inside the pages of the Look and Life Magazines. Nathan was afraid of many things, and this was one more to be added to his list.

Many of the town's mothers had signed the forms to

give their children permission to be part of the "*Pioneer's for Salk*" campaign. Nathan knew his mother would never have considered herself to be un-American. If he were a student now, he knew she'd certainly would have to do her civic duty by pushing Nathan to the front of the line. Nationwide, public schools were joining in the fight to eradicate polio from the world.

"Children, line up quietly and stand single file until it is your turn," Mrs. Brown barked. Nathan began to think of ways he'd try to escape if he was forced to take such a new medication, no matter the good it might be.

Watching as the children fussed and poked one another, he knew no one could possibly care if Nathan Twitters disappeared down the side hallway, out the back door, and escaped to live for the rest of his life in the deep woods of New Jersey. Nathan was relieved that as an adult he didn't have to be forced into this situation. He only had to do his job today and then go to the safety of his apartment.

Seeing these children brought memories to his mind. As a little boy during recess in third grade, he'd always stand by the fence of the school playground. He'd keep his head down, appearing to look for ants crawling on the ground. He always walked quickly to that spot so not to attract too much attention, and only looked up occasionally to see if the teacher was giving her high waving hand, signaling for all the children to return to class after their daily outside exercise break.

Nathan hated those outside breaks because he had to line up with the other children who noisily chatted with one another, and never with him. He seemed to go through life being a part of and yet not a part of life. He did his work in class, answered any questions the teacher shot his way, but most of the time he just kept quiet.

His domineering mother reminded him daily, "Listen to your teachers, but trust no one!" He never knew his father, and his mother wanted him to never make friends because they would leave him eventually, just like his father.

Lunch was very difficult because it was mandatory that all children ate in the cafeteria, and then sat in assigned rows at assigned tables. Nathan had to wait in line in the cafeteria for milk or juice. The tussling children brushing up against him made him uncomfortable.

His mother wouldn't allow him to bring his milk in his lunch box. The reason she forbid this was because he had forgot to drink it one day, he left it in his lunch box and drank it the following day resulting in Nathan throwing up during class, resulting in his mother having to leave her living room in the middle of the day to bring Nathan a change of clothes resulting in her not getting to see what happened to Bill Bauer on her favorite soap opera *Guiding Light*.

When leaving his house in the morning that day, Nathan stood on his stoop and remained stuck thinking about things that got entwined in his brain. He had his lunch box and his books in one hand and a bag of garbage in the other and would have stayed on the stoop forever if his mother hadn't stuck her head out the door each day to simply say, "Move! Come back to earth…. Throw out the garbage, not your lunch." He couldn't really say what he was thinking, but to him it all was all much more important than anything his teachers had to say.

Nathan remembered how school was much too easy for him. He was a very bright child. Not having any friends, he read to escape into worlds and places. After completing fourth grade it all became repetitious to him. He knew his times tables, he could add, multiply, and divide. He had heard the stories about Christopher Columbus and Washington and

Lincoln, all else seemed superfluous. Nathan knew, being a kid, he had no say in the matter, so retreating into his own head made living as he willed possible.

Now seeing those children going single file down the hall, as they were escorted into the huge, cavernous dark auditorium brought all those memories back. There were hundreds of children lining up in front of brown tables, with nurses in crisp white uniforms. Nathan kept his eyes posted on the exit signs, as he watched each child take the tiny paper cup with a sugar cube, and as they were monitored, slid it down their throats. "Move to the front," he managed to mumble to the children. His palms starting to sweat.

Nathan started to think. "This strange sugar cube might kill them. What's in it?" His mind went racing. He felt as if he were going to throw up any second. Mrs. Brown's group was next in line, as his eyes watched them. Nathan started to breath heavily, and as he approached the table to make sure everyone was ok, red bumps began popping out all over his hands, neck and face. "Sir," the nurse asked, "are you ok?" Nathan couldn't speak, he couldn't move. "Sir, sit down, take some water. What's your name?" The nurse in her crisp white uniform escorted him to the nearest seat.

In about thirty minutes, his mother appeared in her overcoat over her nightgown, to the packed auditorium. Her fluffy slippered feet shuffling up the hardwood floors. Her hair in curlers covered with a paisley scarf. The school had her listed as his contact in case of an emergency, which the nurse felt this was.

"Oh, my God! Not again," his mother yelled. All eyes turned to look as she spotted Nathan, taking him forcibly by the arm, scolding him and leading him up the aisles, as she was pushing him forward. All eyes continued following them as Nathan walked solemnly, slowly out the door.

"Nathan, you're not a kid anymore, I can't believe they called me! Calling me at this time of the morning! Don't you dare get sick! Nathan, do you hear me? Not on my new nightgown! Oh, my goodness this is unbelievable. Here I am back at your elementary school! I can't believe this is happening to me, again!" The children laughing and giggling as Miss Brown admonished them and quieted them down.

This was the second time his mother missed the conclusion of her beloved *Guiding Light*.

Chapter 18

Ice Skating With Father Bitner

"Students open your science books to page 30, and we will continue to learn about the life cycle of the earth worm." "Who cares about earth worms", Toby thought. Toby loved to read and learn, but somehow the walls of Woodlake Junior High did not provide her with the knowledge she was searching for.

"Becky, there's a new Elvis film at the Strand," she twisted herself backwards to tell her friend two rows over. As she opened her mouth, a deep throated voice bellowed, "Toby you better head to the principal's office to explain your need to have an outburst at this particular moment!"

"Outburst? I was being as quiet as possible, Mrs. Kaplow." "And while we're on the subject of disrupting this class, Toby please remove those bracelets! Their jangling sounds are too distracting to those who truly wish to learn." Toby adored her collection of bangles. She collected the plastic bangles of every color whenever she entered the Five and Ten in town.

No matter how she tried to express herself and just be Toby, it didn't seem that she could. Especially not in Mrs. Kaplow's classroom.

When the hands of the huge clock over the blackboard inched towards three o'clock, Toby bolted to the door, ran down the hallway, opened the school's front entrance and slid down its railings to escape her weekly prison. Come Friday, Toby was delighted with what lay ahead. Weekends were her best days. Friday night she looked forward to her grandmother's homemade chicken soup, and Saturdays when the snow fell, she would build snow forts with friends, or create snow angels.

November, December, and January were full of snow days when Toby would listen for the loud burst of the fire station's reverberating whistle blowing. Those loud blasts throughout the town signaled that all schools would be closed. Just to be sure, Toby's mother would call Sylvia, who was the attendance secretary at Woodlake Junior High, to double check if in fact Toby could stay home.

St. Mary's Catholic Church on the corner of Madison and 5th was always packed on Sunday mornings, and even for their Sunday afternoon services for those who wanted to stay in bed a few more hours. Toby's mother made sure to get her to the outdoor skating ring across the street from St. Mary's Catholic Church by nine o'clock when she would have time to get around the rink without too many children pushing and shoving. It was at Toby's last birthday that she had begged for her own skates. No longer would she have to wear those awful rentals. Her bright white skates matched her pink and white mittens and woolen hat. She didn't have the ability to do spins yet, but she could get completely around the rink without having to slam into its wooden sides. She felt free rounding each bend, and the frigid air brushing against her skin made her face turn fire engine red.

After dropping off Toby, her mom drove over to Bob's to get a cup of coffee and catch up with the latest goings on of Woodlake. For a few hours, left alone, Toby felt very adult. Here she was circling Woodlake's place to be. This outdoor skating arena where every Woodlake child wanted to be.

The rink was crammed on the weekends. The high school teens stood against the railings, drinking hot chocolate, and flirting; the elementary kids were fearless as they glided and fell, and got up to fall again, and the junior high kids would show off to one another on their latest spins or feats of speed.

There was a time, on very special days, when the lake would freeze over and the kids were allowed to skate its distance from side to side-- but after one of the kids fell into an unforeseen crack in the hardened ice, almost died, and had to have a toe amputated, the township quickly voted on building the Woodlake Municipal Outdoor Skating Arena.

To any outsider, the Woodlake Municipal Outdoor Skating Arena looked quite ordinary--just a large wooden square structure with wooden railings and benches surrounding every side with a small concession stand towards the back for skate rentals, hot chocolate and donuts, but to Toby it was anything but ordinary. It was a the most magical place. During the summer months it remained dormant but come the winter, it quickly transformed.

There were always friends to play ice tag with as everyone whipped across the ice. A few girls could spin round and round, arching their backs like ballerinas. They were the lucky ones who got private lessons from Miss Paula Triplousky. Miss Triplousky had lived in Poland as a young child, and now lived in Woodlake. Along with giving skating and ballet lessons part-time, she also translated information for the Polish immigrants who had begun migrating to this New

Jersey community.

Her friends were but a small part of the excitement, for Toby would be on the lookout for Father Bitner the priest from St. Mary's Catholic Church. He always found time between services to come skate with the town's children. Religion never entered Toby's mind. To her, Father Bitner was just another big kid, a friend to everyone. It seemed amazing that in his long black Cassock rope and flowing hand knitted scarf that he was able to put his tall upright body in such a position to grab hands with the children and form a long chain around the ice.

Father Bitner knew that Toby was Jewish and would never be joining his parish, and yet his greeting to her was equal to everyone else's. "How ya doing there, Toby? Those new skates? They sure are special!" He noticed every detail.

Toby's eyes lit up and began to fixate on Father Bitner's face. His wild bushy hair and eyebrows reminded her of a friendly gnome, although quite tall. His smile was contagious. He took an interest in Toby. He never felt that she was disruptive. He included her in all the activities.

As he circled round, Toby caught hold of one of the boys in the whipping line of children laughing and shouting, "Faster, faster." Toby loved the speed, and reckless nature of the razor-sharp blades digging into the ice. Father Bitner had the ability to get the massive line of kids to change directions, as they bumped up against one another, shrieking and yelling as they rounded the corners. Father Bitner also quickly noticed when things were beginning to get too rough as he blasted out directions, "Everyone off the ice. Take a break on the outside benches. Relax and have some delicious hot chocolate." Toby hated to sit on the wooden benches, but reluctantly obeyed. After ten minutes you could hear Father Bitner's call, "Break is over, everyone back on the ice!"

Moments later, the children sped on with ice chasing, and weaving in and out with Father Bitner at the helm.

Skating with Father Bitner was a weekly ritual for Toby until it all ended one Sunday morning in December, a week before Christmas vacation. Toby was again happily going to the Woodlake Municipal Outdoor Skating Arena. The arena was particularly beautiful at this season because there were two white, huge six-foot snowmen attached to the back wall of the concession stand, and sparkly white snowflakes cut from construction paper, made by Woodlake's elementary children, dangling from red strings everywhere. The gold and silver glitter lit up its drab walls.

Toby quickly ran up the wooden stairs and laced up her now not-so-white skates. As she approached the ice, her friend Linda was coming up the walkway behind her, "Did you hear, Father Bitner's been transferred. At our services, this morning they let everyone know. He won't be joining us anymore."

Toby's face loosened; her mouth dropped open. She couldn't believe it. He one of only a few grownups who understood her. He listened if she was feeling sad. He was never judgmental like most of her teachers.

Toby was almost speechless, but managed to get out the words, "Why?" Linda just shook her head and said, "Don't know, something about being transferred and joining another church in upstate New York." "New York? Just like that? Are you sure?" Toby couldn't calm down.

Toby continued to skate on Sundays, but for her it never seemed the same. With Father Bitner gone the excitement and unfettered joy disappeared with him. Now, it all seemed less frenetic. Toby missed that desperately. Father Bitner's name in the community was mentioned less and less until it was forgotten, but Toby never forgot. He was an adult who accepted her just as she was. No one, except her family, had ever done that before. She forever wondered where he was and how he was doing. Did he think of her and the kids at the Woodlake Municipal Outdoor Skating Arena?

Those questions forever remained unanswered, but she was glad she had known him- even for a little while.

Chapter 19

Woodlake's Last Laugh

D ark sky and dark clouds. Cold descended on Woodlake and in its chill, snow was to follow. Icicles formed on roof overhangs and piles of white blanketing the grass, sidewalks, and swings in the park. Watching the snow as it began to cover all of Woodlake, children pressed their noses against windows, wondering if schools will be closed the next school day. Shop owners were hoping it would stop, not wanting to lose customers who dare not venture out onto the treacherous icy streets. In the warmth of Woodlake's homes, families eat dinner, watch TV, and go to sleep under cozy blankets as the snow continues its onslaught.

Bob sent Rosaline home an hour earlier than usual, not wanting her to get stuck in the diner. As he wiped down the counter and booths, he stopped to call Lilly to see if she was ok; he did not want to leave the diner in case he was needed in the early morning hours when the eggs and milk would be delivered. Bob had never closed the diner for any natural disaster or for any reason. The big hurricane that hit the Jersey shore over thirty years ago and swept its way to Woodlake downing many of the pines, as well as flooding Woodlake's baseball field, hadn't given Bob's dad cause to shut down the diner; this snowstorm would not force Bob to shut its doors either. People depended on the diner in emergencies, for pitchers of hot coffee, sandwiches, and anything else to help the city's workers who kept the town moving.

Bob squeezed into a booth and hunkered down for the night knowing that the morning would be here before he knew it. He didn't even bother to take off his shoes, or his white kitchen apron, just crossed his arms on top of the booth's table. His arms became a temporary pillow and he quickly fell asleep. In the hours that lay ahead, drifts of snow began piling everywhere and power lines began to fall under the weight of the snow. Town's people asleep were unaware until they awoke as the chill began to come into their homes.

Those with electric appliances had no way of making that needed pot of coffee or to turn on the oven to heat up the kitchen. Those lucky enough with gas furnaces could move about in the dark of the morning with the rooms warm and inviting, but the rest who depended on electricity for heat were getting cold and scared. The volunteer fire station's whistle blasted through the town, signaling no school; children were delighted, as parents had to scramble to find out if they were needed on the job.

Most moms were at home, but for those who it was imperative to go out, had to arrange for someone else to watch their children. Rosaline, who lived only blocks from the diner, already had her boots on with scarf, hat, and gloves readied at her front door. She grabbed her heavy coat to trek on over to Bob's. She had momentarily thought about staying under the covers, but Bob would be hammered with people looking for refuge from the blizzard that had finally let up in the early morning hours.

As she opened her front door up the walkway, her beloved Nathan walked up, sloshing through the drifts, smiling as he periodically wiped the light flakes attaching to his glasses.

"I knew you'd be walking over to Bob's and since they closed the schools today, and I am available I didn't want you to walk by yourself. It is rather dangerous out here," he told her. Rosaline felt flattered that Nathan had walked in the dreary morning to accompany her on her short walk over to Bob's.

"Nathan, you didn't have to, but I am certainly glad you did. Why we might even put you to work today. We are going to be swamped with people. The snow always brings everyone out to be together. Let's go, all I need to do is slip on my coat," she said.

They walked hand in hand the three short blocks to Bob's and both enjoyed the silence and beauty of the winter wonderland that had wrapped up Woodlake. Newly together, the clasp of one another's hands felt warm. They savored these intimate moments.

As they stepped into the diner, Bob had already put-up coffee and the aroma permeated everywhere.

"Good to see you, Nathan. Rosaline, everything is up and running. Nathan, ya want some coffee?" Bob asked the couple.

"Hey Bob, is Ginger coming in today? I know her truck might not make it, but Nathan can pitch in if needed, won't you Nathan?" Roseline respectively asked Nathan, not wanting to assume his response.

"Thanks, Nathan," Bob exclaimed, without waiting for a response. Bob knew this was going to be a busy day. "Nathan you can rinse off the dishes and wipe down the tables. Lilly will be in soon to run the register. I think we should be fine. I do appreciate it Nathan, after all you're almost part of the family," he joked.

Nathan blushed, but he knew that Bob meant no harm, and was being inclusive. Bob was a man who spoke his mind at the right moments.

One would think that everyone would stay inside on such a day, but the diner was already starting to buzz. First in were the regulars, all bundled up. Almost unrecognizable. They were wearing layers of sweaters and sweatshirts, faces concealed by woolen caps pulled over their faces and ears.

"Coffee, Rosaline," they said, before they even unburdened themselves, the heaping hot coffee was brought to the booths. Mayor Peeps quickly came in to grab a cup. He would be out in Woodlake surveying the damage, and seeing a few friendly faces made his task a bit more bearable.

"Hi, everyone, we will try and get the streets cleaned up as soon as possible," he randomly said to those chatting in the booths. It was evident that at this early in the morning, just being warm and safe was all that anyone cared about, but Mayor Peeps felt it necessary to display his civic duty. Next in was Buzz, who knew that many of the pines that he felt protective of were in need of dusting off the heavy layers of snow that might cause damage to their branches. Buzz, was the protector of the trees in Woodlake.

"Hey, Bob it is cold out there. Can't believe how much has fallen in twelve short hours? Every inch of Woodlake is powdered like a wedding cake. Just hope people get their power soon," Buzz said. He was always the one to move at a clip, he gulped down a rather large cup of hot coffee and left just as quick as he entered.

The diner was certainly awake, despite the gridlock of Woodlake's streets. Even Nathan, who never had been behind the counter, was blending in well. He loved being near Rosaline and rushing in and out of the backroom readying the dishes, cups, silverware, and glasses that were coming in and out of the kitchen to be washed for the customers that found refuge within Bob's protective walls. As schools had closed, moms with kids walked in to slosh through and have a cup of hot chocolate and a stack of the best pancakes in town. The onslaught of blustering white flakes wasn't deterring the Woodlake townsfolk from making life as normal as usual. Those without power at home had decided that it was better to wait it out at Bob's rather than risk the severe dipping temperatures.

The volunteer fire department was on the alert with blankets and hoped that candles illuminating darkened homes didn't tilt over and cause everything to catch fire. Even those safely lit pent-up fireplaces, that were merely decorative and only used yearly to hold Christmas stockings might go ablaze. A responsible homeowner, assigned to watch the dancing flames, could accidentally nod off to sleep under the welcoming warmth and suddenly those drifting embers could leap upon the living room curtains unnoticed.

This niveous town of Woodlake was adjusting to the sensory overload. It was aware that it was temporary, yet they loved embracing nature's sudden shake-up. By afternoon, snow men were appearing on front yards. Snow angel patterns were stamped onto covered walkways. Snowballs were flying, and the loud blowing of large city trucks plowing the streets could be heard. As the trucks pushed ahead clearing roadways, fortresses appeared up against curbs for girls and boys to hide behind.

By late afternoon, the snow had stopped. Many shop owners finally got to reopen their doors, but only for a few hours. Children earning a few dollars from shoveling walkways were tired, and those having lunch at Bob's, after sitting there from breakfast on, were ready to return to their homes. Mayor Peeps had recently returned to let everyone know that power was on in most houses, and school would reopen in the morning.

Bob decided to take a small break and dragged Lilly outside to see the wonderland before the black slush that would follow would make it look bleak. "Oh, Bob, it's too cold, wait my scarf," she said as he pulled her down the steps. She laughed as he hurried her along the pathways and circled the block until they quickly returned to the diner.

Nathan and Rosaline came to the doorway too and all four stood for a moment looking out into the street. "Ok, that's enough of a break, back to work," Bob chuckled but not before holding Lilly tightly, as he roguishly planted a kiss on her lips.

Woodlake chuckled back, as tiny magical snowflakes began to fall again.

Chapter 20

Snow Days

The diner was quiet, as was the town of Woodlake until the long raucous blare of the firehouse siren could be heard in every household, indicating today would be a snow day for all the children. It had snowed heavily through the night and into the early morning hours making the movement of school buses and cars an impossibility.

Each child almost simultaneously leaped out of bed pressing their noses to the nearest windows. Small hands and large hands wiped the haze off those windows to squint to see outside in the early morning darkness as the flakes continued to fall everywhere. The tree branches started bowing from the weight of each tiny white crystal piling one on top another.

Already kneeling by her bedroom window gazing at the wonder of it all, Toby was ready to venture outdoors. In her mind she was ready to build the biggest snow man ever seen in the town of Woodlake, as well as a fort and make snow angels.

"Mom, are you up? I will be dressed in five minutes. Cereal and toast," she yelled out her door. Although, it was pitch dark in the house and outside, Toby was wide awake and ready to venture into her frost laden yard. On most school days her mother would have to pry her out of bed, while pushing her limp body into the bathroom to wash up, eat breakfast and get herself ready to catch the school bus at eight—not so today.

Toby heard no response to her loud demands. She knew how to prepare cereal and toast, but in such darkness, Toby was aware that playing outside would have to wait.

Bob, on the other hand, had already dressed and was bundled up in his blue woolen pea jacket, gloves, boots and knit cap to take the snowy walk to the diner in case the folks of Woodlake needed refuge from the storm. He decided to let Lilly sleep in and would pass by Rosaline's home to see if she would accompany him to get ready just in case some regulars stopped by for their usual coffee.

Woodlake went from being a place of traffic jams, kids on bicycles, women pushing strollers, Tom Hankins the police chief patrolling the streets, Sidney delivering milk, children waiting for school buses to arrive, others walking to classes, and now-- to a complete stand still. This blanketing of white transformed everything and everyone. Life seemed to suddenly stop.

"Mom, are you up yet?" Toby yelled out after an hour of patiently sitting, starring through the steamy window. The sun was beginning to peak through the grey, black clouds. In her bathrobe and slippers, Toby's mom finally entered her bedroom and plopped onto her daughter's bed smiling. "I see you are already dressed, how come?" she joked. "Did you brush your teeth?" Toby feverishly shook her head and gently pulled her mom down the steps to the kitchen.

A second time, the firehouse siren rang out its penetrating high-pitched blare, in case sleeping parents or children hadn't heard the first one. Several times during the winter, such storms hit Woodlake. Every child in Woodlake lived for such moments. After that belting noise, any child who moments before might have had a cold, might have felt reticent to attend school that day, or would amble very slowly out their front doors and slowly up the school steps, were quickly dressed and ready to hit the streets. Parents who wanted to stay indoors were coerced out of their warm beds to ready their children to go out into the frozen wonderland.

After slurping down a glass of milk, shoveling her cereal into her mouth, and stuffing toast down her throat, Toby begged and was finally allowed outside. As she pushed open the front door, which wasn't easy with snow having piled on it through the night, she was greeted by her friend Linda. Linda too was bundled up in her snow suit, woolen hat, gloves, boots and a scarf her sister made for her last Christmas that had flecks of silver, which seemed to glimmer. Like radar, the two friends knew where each other would be, especially under these conditions. As they looked at one another, "Snow angels," screamed out of their mouths simultaneously, and the two fell flat on their backs into the snow waving their arms back and forth to make the impression of heavenly wings imprinted there for all to see. It was penetratingly frigid, but neither cared nor even expressed concern.

Back at the diner, Bob had the coffee going and the kitchen's ovens were awaiting the first arrivals. Rosaline made sure all the salt and pepper shakers were filled and that the napkin holders were ready to go. The Woodland Daily Gazette had somehow been dropped off as usual, and they were readied on the counter for takers. Bob wanted to be sure that Woodlake's regulars could continue their routines as always.

Life in this small town, through all the seasons, had a sameness that Bob adhered to and loved. As the snow continued to fall, Toby and Linda continued to play, as had children before them. Suddenly, at that exact moment, a secret pact was being made with the universe that all would stay the same and never change.

Yet, we all knew the truth.

Chapter 21

The White Sisters

At the junior high school, for twenty-five years Miss White directed the young women of Woodlake, in her Home Economics class, on the fineries of running a household. Her mother had circled the ad in Woodlake's weekly paper, handed it to her daughter, told her directly and without cause, "Charlene you need to move out, and get a job." She drove her daughter over to Woodlake for an interview, and she waited in the car until her daughter came out with her signed contract. Her oldest daughter had received a fine education at the local college and was quite capable in being able to teach young ladies how to cook, sew, and set up their future households. Her youngest daughter, Roanne, was slow and awkward and had been taken out of school many years ago to live at home with the family. The job advertisement said an apartment over the teaching quarters was included, and Miss White's mother envisioned both of her daughters leaving her home together. And, so it was, that

Miss Charlene White and her younger sister Roanne left their mother's home and never returned.

Charlene White received her weekly teacher's salary and was able to provide her and her sister with food, clothing, and their daily needs. On weekends, they both would come downstairs and sit in the make shift kitchen that the students used during the day to learn how to cook. The two sisters would pretend that they lived in this large grand home with the white organza curtains that Charlene had sewn and put up many years ago when she first moved into the small apartment upstairs with Roanne. When the students left for the day, both sisters would quietly sit in the kitchen and have their dinner alone. No one ever came to visit.

Odd indeed was the fact that these two sisters would live out their remaining years in the upstairs apartment of Woodlake's Public-School annex, but never the less, it was so.

During the day when Charlene taught the girls, Roanne would often peek downstairs to watch the students make cream cheese or tuna sandwiches and see them basting their organza aprons. She would stand on the landing and just stare. She never spoke. She quietly watched, hands in the pockets of her long grey sweater that almost reached to her knees; she was smiling at times, and at other times giggling to herself, although no one knew why.

While Roanne was very quiet and shy, Charlene was quite the talker. She gave long laborious instructions to the girls on how to place the pins evenly on their sewing projects, how to spread the tuna dip carefully, or the dos and don'ts of setting a table.

"Now ladies, watch as I place the knife, spoon, and fork on this napkin. Ladies pay attention to the word FORKS, the order goes left to right: F for fork, O for the shape of the plate, K for knives, and S for spoons. R... well forget that letter." The girls just rolled their eyes. Charlene White took her job extremely serious, and she expected the students to share the same intensity she had.

"Ladies, watch as I carefully place the pins along the bias of this apron. Evenly place the pins along the seam line and let the machine glide across its seams. Girls are you watching?" interrogating them, "Remember if they are not straight, you will have to rip them out again." Again, the girls would roll their eyes because no matter how straight the placement of their pins, it was never to Miss White's liking. Again and again, she would demand they pull out the seams and very few ever completed an apron to meet her specifications.

She never taught class without her white oxfords polished to perfection in the springtime, and her black oxfords in the winter. Her crisp white blouse was always perfectly pressed, and a sweater hung precisely squared on her shoulders held on with a polished gleaming silver clip.

She made sure to strut back and forth, hands crossed behind her back, barking orders, and watching as each girl worked in pairs setting tables, or eyeing each sandwich as the girls mixed carefully measured ingredients of cream cheese and raisins.

"Ladies I've noticed that very few of you have completed your aprons, if they aren't ready by Christmas, we will have to start all over again until they are," she said.

One day, on an early December morning, and for no apparent reason, Barbara Belson, a student in Miss White's class, whispered to her friends nearby about Miss White's younger sister Roanne, "That Roanne is just plain creepy. She lurks about watching us and I wish she'd stay upstairs where she belongs. She smells."

The others had never thought much about Roanne. She

was usually quiet and stood off to the side by herself. Her short, wispy blond hair was pulled off her face with a pink bow. She always wore Mary-jane shoes with short white socks. She was probably about forty years old, yet had the demeanor of a child. If Barbara Belson hadn't pointed it out to them, they might have forgotten she was in the room.

Roanne had never done anyone any harm. As a little girl she had spent most days alone in her room, and her sister Charlene rarely talked to her. As a child Charlene had always obeyed her mother's word, "The less Roanne is seen, the less problems you will have. She isn't very smart and out of sight will be better for all of us."

For some reason, many years ago, Roanne accidently wandered downstairs while her older sister was teaching the girls. Over time she had become a fixture in Miss While's home economics' classes. A fixture that everyone accepted, even Charlene. After all, Charlene had no other family, other than her baby sister, and after a while, began to appreciate and love her sister's presence. She knew that her sister was different. It was fine.

No one ever seemed to complain until that Barbara Belson started those whisperings and those whisperings seemed to travel quite fast. As soon as she opened her mouth, the other girls began to listen. Like a bolt of lightning, her words traveled among the girls that things weren't quite right with Roanne White. None of the girls knew for sure what in fact was her problem. None of them had cared before, but somehow Barbara and her talk caught their attention.

"Yes, did you see how she watches us as we walk past her? She doesn't bathe, and I've never seen her wash her hands before she picks up the food. She doesn't belong here. Let's get her out," Barbara would say.

And just like that, as if everyone was listening, on a cold

winter morning two weeks before the Christmas holiday vacation, Charlene White was summoned to the Principal's office. How was it possible after twenty-five years that Miss White would come to this? Miss White feared for her job. During her illustrious teaching profession, she never had been told to dismiss the girls early on a Friday afternoon.

She felt it must be serious. Miss White quickly grabbed her checkered woolen jacket, and scarf, and gently led Roanne upstairs and told her, sternly, to wait in her room until she returned. She then hurried across the street to the steps of Woodlake Junior High. She was extremely concerned. There was no place for her and her sister to return to. Her mother had died last year, and she nor Roanne had received any part of their mother's insurance. It all went to their mother's second husband who they saw from afar at their mother's funeral.

"I am always on time, I have never taken a sick day, I take accurate attendance, what could it be," Miss white wondered. She didn't know what had gone wrong. Roanne had been joining the students for years, so that couldn't be it, or could it?

Sitting on the bench outside the principal's office made her feel like a little kid who had done something wrong.

"Miss White, you can come inside now," Principal Ribner's secretary summoned.

"Miss White have a seat." And she did.

Miss White realized that she was beginning to sweat rapidly, and awkwardly took off her jacket and scarf. She wasn't sure if it was the heat making her uncomfortable or being inside Principal Ribner's office.

"Miss White I am sure you are wondering why I have asked you here today. It has come to my attention that your sister Roanne has been making some of the girls in your class uncomfortable," Principal Ribner said.

With that, Miss White's face turned aside, and she found it hard to hold back her tears and shock. She was about to speak, but before she had a chance to open her mouth Principal Ribner continued, "That Barbara Belson is one troublemaker. In the past several months, she and her parents have visited my office over ten times for a variety of reasons. First there was the janitor who she claimed used foul language in the hallway. Next the cafeteria woman who her parents said barely speaks English, and the crossing guard who they claimed drank on the job. It seemed before they had one complaint another was close behind. I wanted you here early before everyone left for the weekend to let you know I appreciate how you have helped our girls at Woodlake Junior High. I know you can be tough and strict, but don't worry you won't be having any problems from Barbara Belson or her parents ever again. I have seen to that!"

Miss White tried to listen. What was he saying? He hadn't mentioned what would be happening to her and her sister. She had never thought of retiring. Teaching was all she had. This was her life. This was her home.

Not hearing all his words Charlene blurted out, "Mr. Ribner, I do appreciate your support. I will keep Roanne, my sister upstairs in our apartment, I promise she will never be an issue again. She means no harm."

"Miss White," Mr. Ribner rapidly jumped in, "Roanne reminds me so much of my younger daughter who attends a special school in Bricklake. My daughter is learning and growing so much. I'd love to have her meet Roanne some afternoon. They also have a class for adults, and you might want to take your sister there one day and, one more thing. I want Roanne to keep attending your classes. Do you understand?"

"Yes, Mr. Ribner. I do," Miss White said with relief.

"And, please join us next week in the teacher's lounge for our annual Christmas pot luck. We never see you over here. Please make that tuna spread with raisins that the students always complain about. I know they might not like it, but I tasted it secretly and it's delicious," Principal Ribner said.

"Oh", he paused with great reverence, "by the way, don't forget to bring Roanne."

Chapter 22

Our Little Secret

Chorus practice in Woodlake Junior High was loud. As everyone filed in, the chairs had to be arranged in perfect rows scraping the floors as they were dragged up onto the risers; next, the students searched for their folders and music sheets that were piled high on Mr. Tenzer's, the choir director, desk. While each singer arranged their music sheets in their folders according to the order Mr. Tenzer had written on the blackboard, the sopranos and altos shifted to the left and the tenors and basses to the right. Some sat and others stood talking and adjusting their metal music stands until Mr. Tenzer stood tapping his baton lightly. In his crisp white shirt, black bowtie, and tweed jacket, that faint tapping sound brought all eyes front, and silence descended on the room.

"We will start with A Mighty Fortress. Sopranos will begin with the melody," he said. Beatrice Swanson always got the solo. "No matter how hard the altos belted out the harmonies no one seemed to notice them," Toby thought. Beatrice Swanson always hit those notes that no one even could come close to. Afterwards, at the school concerts, she received the applause.

It was just two weeks before Woodlake Junior High School's Annual Christmas Choral and Band Concert when Beatrice Swanson came down with a case of the chicken pox. There could be nothing worse for Mr. Tenzer's star performer. There was no quick cure, no chance of hiding her sudden malady, and too many tickets sold for a cancelation. Mr. Tenzer had a wonderful, trained chorus, but now he was beginning to feel it all seemed hopeless. What could he do? After months of practice the coveted performer was sick with no chance of returning until her case of chicken pox ran its course.

There was Jenny Louis, also a fine soprano, but she was afraid to look at the audience. Every time she saw the hundreds of eyes focused on her, she choked. Beatrice, on the other hand, knew how to connect with the crowd. While fluttering her eyelids and folding her hands angelically into her white dress, she mesmerized everyone. Toby, in her deep alto tones, was forever told to quiet down so as not to drown out Beatrice. Toby was glad that Beatrice got sick. No matter how hard her section tried, it never seemed to please Mr. Tenzer.

"Now ladies, we need to hear that pulsating beat, but make sure to tone it down when the sopranos are bringing forth the melody. Toby, you are doing a great job but try not to overpower Beatrice on the first stanza," Mr. Tenzer said.

"Yes, Mr. Tenzer. I'm sorry Mr. Tenzer. I won't do it again Mr. Tenzer," Toby said.

"The heck with Beatrice and her angelic voice. What about me," Toby couldn't help but think to herself. "Beatrice this and Beatrice that," she continued to think.

There was that talent contest held at downtown's Strand Movie Theater several years before when Beatrice and Toby were pitted against one another. Woodlake was holding its Diamond Jubilee. It began with a beauty contest. All the young woman paraded across the theater's stage in bathing suits. They were a bevy of loveliness. All had their large bouffant hairdos piled to the rafters and teetered across the stage in the highest heels they could balance on. The winner got to be part of the panel that would judge the talent contest. Wearing her Diamond Jubilee crown and evening gown, she sat with the Mayor and the city council to judge the contestants.

First, there was little Eddie Beltz who did his tap-dancing routine that he had practiced all summer at the Y's Tap Your Way to Stardom classes. Next Pauline Gotier did her acrobatics bending to the left and to the right as her mother snapped picture after picture with her Brownie camera, blocking everyone in the rows behind her. At last, were the two girls ready for their showdown. Toby had been practicing for weeks with her mother, who was able to play the tune on their piano.

She had decided to sing You're a Grand Old Flag after seeing Yankee Doodle Dandy on the Million Dollar Movie hundreds of times. She had seen it enough times to copy James Cagney's gait and panache. She had saved the paper top hat from the July 4th Pageant. It was red, white, and blue with hundreds of gold stars that she had pasted on one by one until every inch of it was covered. Her grandmother had sewn a patriotic costume that glittered from every angle.

She was so ready to wow the crowd with her loud and belting rendition. She had every move memorized from the soldier-like salute out to the audience, the waving of a small

American flag tucked into her side, and the marching-like send off. This would bring everyone to their feet. There was no way she wasn't going to win and win big!

Toby came onto the stage and signaled to her mom who played the introduction. Toby got all the notes out perfectly. She marched up and down the stage, waving her flag as everyone rose to their feet cheering. Toby felt she had dominated the stage and the prize was hers, but as the applause died down, the lights dramatically dimmed and a spotlight that Beatrice's dad borrowed from his brother, who worked for a small theater in the next town over, shown onto a flatbed wagon covered in crinkled pink organza. Beatrice's uncle and dad pulled the wagon onstage. Upon the slowly moving wagon, Beatrice was in a floor length white gown covered in blue crystals. She had angel wings covered in cotton balls attached to her back and elbow length white gloves. Her blond hair was aglow with finger curls dangling all over her head. No one in Woodlake had ever seen the likes of this. To make it worse, when Beatrice opened her mouth to sing Somewhere Over the Rainbow, there wasn't a sound in the theater. As Beatrice's cousin June, who played piano for the Woodlake church, began to play, Beatrice's voice sweetly floated towards the onlookers. Beatrice ended to perfection as June played her final note. Toby knew it was all over. Beatrice politely curtsied, trying to balance herself as she was pulled off stage. The auditorium erupted. Beatrice returned modestly taking another bow.

When the talent trophies were handed out, and Toby came in second to Beatrice's first place, it was no surprise. Still, it was a huge disappointment. She had practiced long and hard and had done every move perfectly. Yet it wasn't enough. Perhaps with Beatrice's case of the chicken pox, Toby might, at long last, get a small consolation prize for all that hard work. She wasn't sure if her alto voice could come to the rescue, but it was worth a try.

Monday approached, and it was eight days before the Christmas concert was to take place. The choir room had paper chains of varying colors hanging from the bulletin boards and doorway. Mr. Tenzer had agonized over the weekend about how things would work out.

"As you know, our own Beatrice Swanson won't be with us this year due to her recent outbreak of the chicken pox and I have thought what we could do," Mr. Tenzer told the class, "I was wondering if one of you would be willing to work a little harder for the next seven days and learn her part. We can make things work by...." In midsentence, Toby jumped up out of her seat, waving her hand high in the air. She had such enthusiasm that Mr. Tenzer was amazed, "Why Toby I haven't even finished my proposal."

"Mr. Tenzer I would be more than happy to work hard. I can stay after school, and you know my mother plays piano and would be more than happy to assist me," she blurted out without even discussing any of this with her mom. Toby was determined to seize this moment before it had a chance to pass her by, or worse that anyone else stepped in to fill the spot that she so desperately wanted.

Mr. Tenzer's mouth fell open, not sure what to say. He knew Toby could sing, but she was loud and didn't have the delicacy of his prized Beatrice. Again, Toby struck, "Mr. Tenzer just give me the music tonight and I promise by tomorrow I will know it. Please, I promise I won't let you or our choir down." With that Mr. Tenzer was dumbfounded and couldn't say no.

"Ok, Toby, but tomorrow I will listen to you and if you aren't up to this challenge, I must go with someone else. Do you understand," he asked her.

"Yes, Mr. Tenzer I will not disappoint you."

As the bell, went off signaling the end of choir practice, Toby went to the podium and Mr. Tenzer handed her the two songs that Beatrice would have been singing solo while the choir sang as backup. She had mouthed the words since September for each and every practice and felt taking over Beatrice's solo was doable. Their voices were different, but Toby knew she could win Mr. Tenzer's affection.

Arriving home, she went straight into the kitchen where her mom was getting dinner ready.

"Mom you've got to help me tonight. This is my chance to prove to Mr. Tenzer and the entire Woodlake Junior High Choir that I can sing. Mom please we can eat peanut butter and jelly sandwiches tonight, please, please!" "Alright, the food is almost done, what is so important? Mr. Tenzer knows you can sing. Why else would he have picked you to sing in the school's choir?" "Mom, the solo. Beatrice is sick and she won't be able to sing the solo like she does every year. It could be my chance this year."

"Beatrice, sick?" her mother said with concern.

"Just the chicken pox, not too serious. What'd ya say, mom can we practice now? I have the music. Mr. Tenzer will try me out tomorrow and I want to be ready."

With that, Toby's mother lowered the temperature on the tuna casserole baking in the oven and headed to the living room, where she would accompany her daughter on the black upright that she loved fantasizing herself playing at Carnegie Hall while she played. The music was simple enough for her to play, but solos soared up so high that Toby's voice couldn't come close. Unfortunately, she wasn't able, by any means, to make her low timber like voice rise into the lilt of Beatrice's soprano renderings. Her mother sadly knew this.

"This isn't going to work, Toby. You have to understand

that each of us are different with our own special gifts. You have the difficult, but wonderful, job of supporting the melodies," her mother told her.

Toby wasn't consoled by her mother's words and asked to be excused from dinner after thanking her for helping. She hoped that she could magically will herself a case of the chicken pox by morning. She didn't want to face Mr. Tenzer, and definitely not any of the choir members.

Awaking the next morning, Toby knew missing school was not an option. As she slowly walked to school, she dreaded facing Mr. Tenzer and all her friends and listening to him explain why she couldn't take over for his precious Beatrice. As she was mindlessly walking down the corridor, she crashed into Mr. Tenzer rounding the hallway. A towering stack of music sheets he was holding flew into the air, Toby was startled and began to cry.

"Oh, Mr. Tenzer I didn't mean to. Don't worry. I'll pick up the sheet music for you. I'm sorry," And then it all tumbled out of her mouth, "I tried to sing like Beatrice, I know I have been a big disappointment. My mom was practicing with me last night for hours, but my voice couldn't hit those high notes." Her tears flowed in torrents.

"Hey, Toby calm down," he said.

As he pulled his handkerchief out of his coat pocket and handed it to Toby, he continued to reassure her.

"You haven't been a disappointment. You have a lovely voice. Our alto section would be lost without your leadership and enthusiasm. I didn't know if you could handle those solos because of the different range both of your voices have, but I never doubted your ability. Relax, it will all work out. Now go in the bathroom and wipe that face of yours and I will expect you in the choir room in five minutes."

Toby turned and dashed into the girl's room, wiped her

face, and was sitting in her seat within three minutes flat. The rehearsal was going well, and as they approached the solo, Toby wasn't sure what was coming but as she glanced at Mr. Tenzer swinging his baton, he motioned for her to stand.

Up she stood and Mr. Tenzer signaled to the pianist, Jerome, who was an honor's band student at Woodlake Junior High. Mr. Tenzer momentarily halted everyone and whispered something to Jerome. Next, Jerome began his introduction to Silent Night as Mr. Tenzer pointed his baton at Toby who sang out each note to perfection. The choir chimed in with their humming and beautiful harmonies. Toby sat down dumbfounded. Mr. Tenzer nodded to Toby that she had done a wonderful job. The final solo went just as well, and some of her friends even patted her on the back for a job well done as they filed out the door.

"I don't understand Mr. Tenzer?" Toby questioned her teacher before leaving the room. "Last night it was horrible, awful but today?" "Well Toby, I know your mom loves you very much but I'm sorry to say she isn't the best of piano players. I just told Jerome to lower your key when you got up to sing and I knew you would do fine. I never doubted it for a minute. It can be our little secret."

Spontaneously, Toby lifted herself on her tip toes and gave Mr. Tenzer a huge hug. He was very embarrassed.

Toby turned to leave but not before repeating, "Yes, Mr. Tenzer, our little secret."

Chapter 23

Lilly's Child

Small town life could be stifling, and Woodlake was no exception. There was one elementary school, one junior high, and one high school. The main downtown area could be circled in ten minutes. Whatever your choice, the Strand to catch a movie, or go for a walk in the large city park, the best place to catch up on gossip or just relax before the busy work week began was, hands down, Bob's Diner.

The diner was, in actuality, not a diner at all. One might say it was a luncheonette, a local hangout, restaurant, but Bob's dad always referred to it as a diner, and it stuck. Not shaped like a railroad car, as The American Heritage Dictionary defined "Diner," for whatever reason, it was never thought of as anything else. It didn't have a rounded outside exterior, with shiny silver chrome, nor could it ever be moved from its current location.

Bob's was box-shaped, with a brown shingled roof, and two large entrance doors that probably were salvaged from a bank or perhaps a library. It was painted many colors over the years, but now the exterior was a very bright red, and on the brown shingled roof was a very oversized sign that simply read in bright pink neon, "Bob's Diner" that flashed on and off day and night. There were matching pink window boxes that adorned the large picture windows, and when the weather was good, a variety of flowers overflowed in them. Usually on the windows were all kinds of signs announcing local town activities, "Library Reading Saturdays at 1 PM", "Spaghetti dinner at the YMCA sponsored by the Girl Scouts", and recently, "Skating Lessons".

The inside was rather inviting. An old bronze cash register welcomed customers before they sat down, and sometimes Lilly, Bob's wife, would help by taking customers' checks. There was a large counter with stools that spun, and booths flanked either side of the diner. Bob was able to watch all the comings and goings from the kitchen which looked out into the diner. Old juke boxes were still in working order, and often the teenagers loved listening to the music along with the older regulars that stopped by two or three times a week. Over the huge entrance doors hung a large black and white clock, like the ones often found in school classrooms.

During the morning hours, especially weekends, Bob's Diner was the place to be. It had been around since the Second World War, and Bob had inherited it from his dad since none of his brothers wanted to be stuck in this small town. He had met Lilly, his wife, on the playground of the only elementary school in town, they went on to the only junior high school, went steady throughout high school and married two weeks after they both graduated. It was Bob n' Lilly or Lilly n' Bob. Their names forever joined as one sound. "There's Bob n' Lilly," someone might say, "How's ya doing Lilly n' Bob?"

Bob had hung out for hours upon hours in the kitchen after school, so when his dad died suddenly one morning before the breakfast crowd arrived, running it now seemed quite natural. He could scramble an egg in two minutes flat, keep several pans going at the same time, and people came from far and near for his beef stew. Lilly felt pride knowing that her husband was such a respected man in the community. She was his dutiful wife, kept the house clean, raked the leaves, and although wanting to give him a family, was unable to have any children.

She would often come to the diner in the afternoon, sometimes hang out in the backroom, or assist at the register and watch the high school kids come in for their weekly burgers and fries. She liked to fantasize about one of the kids being hers and helping them with their homework or assisting them with their scouting projects. Bob was such a good provider, yet she always felt that she had fallen short of being able to make him a father. Bob never wanted for much, he had the diner and Lilly, and was so glad whenever she came by to surprise him.

On one very busy Sunday morning, The Woodlake Gazette's Sunday Edition had a story that caught Lilly's eye on its second page: at the Woodlake Church, Wednesday evening, Reverend Jones found a small baby bundled up in its main sanctuary. Parents unknown. Anyone knowing of such a birth please contact Officer Jones at the Woodlake Police Station.

Immediately, Lilly thought about her and Bob coming forth and like she'd seen in the movies, taking that child, and raising it as their own. He or she might be a wonderful edition to their family. Their newly found child could take over the diner when Bob retired, and she and Bob would have many grandchildren to care for in their old age. Lilly imagined every last detail. Even the big wedding that she and Bob would throw for this tiny baby when it grew up and found his or her true love. Perhaps, decorating the diner, and Bob of course catering it, while Rosaline and Ginger would assist in serving the food.

She was getting way ahead of herself, but she had thought of these moments for many years. Oh yes, her head spun in so many directions, she would have to call Sheriff Brown and let him know that they would be more than happy to be first on the list, albeit she knew how sad it was that the, "poor thing had been abandoned in such a heartless way..."

Lilly wanted to rush out the door, but she couldn't at this moment because the customers were advancing like storm troopers. Come ten o'clock on Sundays, at Bob's, everyone was vying for a seat in the diner. It had become a ritual in Woodlake. Either attend early mass and eat breakfast at Bob's, sleep in late then eat breakfast at Bob's, or sleep very very late and have brunch at Bob's and the heck with church.

This Sunday was no busier than any other. Of course, one couldn't predict how the day would go, but as Sundays usually went it was guaranteed to have large crowds. Lilly made sure Bob could handle the register for an hour or so, and when he agreed, she went off to speak to Officer Jones.

This could be the sign that Lilly had been praying about. A baby right in our small town of Woodlake. Bob n' Lilly would be the perfect parents; Lilly knew this in her heart. She had wanted to tell Bob before dashing over to the police station, but it would be just the surprise he needed, and she didn't want to ruin it. She didn't need to drive or take a bus, because if she walked quickly the station was but three short blocks from the diner.

Woodlake town center consisted of a ten-block area. There was Main Street, which contained the Strand Movie

Theater, the Woodlake Police Station, a large Five and Ten, Swartz's Toy Store, White's Music Store, The Spot -- where one could pick up the Woodlake Daily Gazette, buy candy, comic books, and magazines --, Phil's Grocery, and Evangeline's Hair Salon. Bob's Diner was three blocks south of Main Street near the Woodlake High School, and Junior High. Over on Clifton Avenue was the Clifton Avenue Grade School, next to the Woodlake Public Library. There was also the YMCA, and two towns over, about a thirty-minute drive, was the Jersey Township Hospital. When true emergencies arouse, the volunteer fire department would rev up the solitary fire truck, and within ten minutes most alarms were answered. Dora's kitchen might have burnt down that one time, when most of the volunteers were attending a local wedding; but luckily, she had heard about putting salt over the flames, and it worked.

Lilly finally approached the police station. She didn't hesitate. Before barging into the station she replayed the story in her head of wanting to be a mother. It wasn't enough being a wife. A wife took care of her husband and her children. That's what she was taught as a child and today she might be able to fulfill her dreams. It surely would take lots of adjustments, but she felt certain she was ready to be a mom.

She was greeted by Officer Jones who was somewhat perplexed and concerned to see Lilly away from the diner on a Sunday afternoon. "Everything ok Lilly n' Bob?" "Yes," Lilly responded, "Can I speak to you? It's extremely important that we speak NOW!" Officer Jones rapidly stepped aside to let Lilly pass and waited until she took a seat in his office. She couldn't wait for him to be seated.

"That baby you found," blurting out her words. "Uh, is it possible, could it be possible, I mean us? Could Bob and I be the parents? You know we're decent and reliable." Trying to weigh his words carefully he spoke, "Oh, Lilly, the mom came forward. She showed up here. She had second thoughts and took it home. I'm sorry. I mean these things happen," he bluntly responded, not knowing how to make it any easier. He knew how much Lilly had wanted a child. In Woodlake, nothing stayed a secret for long.

"Thanks, Jim, I thought maybe it was a sign," trying to shirk it off. Not wanting Jim to feel poorly.

Lilly quickly perked up, as was her nature. "Thanks, Jim, for taking the time from your busy day. Don't worry. I guess it's all as it should be," She tersely hugged him, and left.

Rather than returning to the diner, Lilly decided to stop in at the Spot before it closed at three to pick up a movie magazine. Reading about Hollywood's problems might be an easy distraction for a moment. There were bicycles piled up out front, and old man Hankins was flaying his arms at the kids' reading the comics that they didn't intend to pay for. Lilly headed towards the back of the store where the magazines sat on racks, and she saw Carmela, Carmen's daughter thumbing through teen magazines. She had gone to visit her aunt for several months; but the rumor was that she got knocked up by Benny and had to leave town for nine months.

Lilly had seen Benny and Carmela come into the diner often, months ago and they seemed like a couple in love, but ever since Carmela had returned to Woodlake, Benny came in with some other girl. He never looked back.

"How ya doing Carmela, glad you're back in town," Lilly cautiously asked, not wanting to appear as if she was prying. Since, Lilly had to bypass Carmela on her way to the magazine racks, it was the polite thing to do.

Carmela had been back in town for over two months now,

and Lilly was the first person who seemed to care, Carmela thought. Her leaving town and returning happened without anyone seeming to be interested.

She was holding everything in, her insides were ready to burst like when her baby pushed out. Her mother never mentioned it to her, her friends stopped talking to her, and she just wanted to scream. "I'm not invisible, doesn't anyone see me. Truly see me?" Carmela thought. The pain that Carmela felt was unbearable.

Without a lot of prethought, Carmela lurched forward and grabbed ahold of Lilly and wept. Lilly turned around to see if any of this was noticed. Old Mr. Henkins was too busy shooing the kids out the door, and the kids were too busy running everywhere. Lilly wanted to let Carmela go, but Carmela held on so tight that Lilly decided to forgo the magazine and directed her outside.

"Carmela, it's going to be ok. Come with me," Lilly started to sooth her without knowing why. She directed her onto a bench nearby in front of a fountain lining the sidewalk.

Carmela didn't hold back but heaved and sobbed. "The baby I signed it away, my mom said I couldn't keep it...." More crying. Lilly had heard such rumors when Carmela returned from her trip to her aunt.

"I didn't stay with my aunt. It was all a lie. I was put in a home for wayward girls. It was awful," with more tears falling like buckets of rain. Lilly was at a loss for words, and with wide eyes soaked in all of Carmela's words.

"I know things will never be the same for you, but you will be ok, I will see to that," Lilly assured her.

This was not the child that Lilly had planned on, but why not? "I can be there for her, I will be there for her," Lilly decided.

"Let's go to the movies, my treat," Lilly tenderly spoke.

"We can call your mom to let her know you are ok."

Carmela sniffed, wiped her eyes, and nodded, yes.

"We can stop at Bob's after, and I will get Rosaline to serve you the biggest and best milkshake you have ever had." Lilly gently put her arm around Carmela's shoulder, and they both walked towards the Strand.

"Thanks, so much, thanks so much," Carmela squealed. "And popcorn, too?" "Yes," Lilly gladly said, "anything for you, anything for you."

Chapter 24

The Spot

M r. Henkins spent half his time reading the newspapers that arrived from the surrounding townships, the other half trying to get kids out of his small but popular business called The Spot. Mr. Henkins had been the proprietor for decades and before that, his parents were. He rented one of the apartments upstairs to Mr. Twitters, and he lived with his wife in the other one. The Spot was the place to hang out for a while, catch up with friends, and connect. Those who needed to get in touch with someone might use the pay phone located in the back of the tiny establishment.

There were floor to ceiling racks of publications. There was something for everyone: food, health, history, sports, women's issues, fashion, daily, monthly, young, old, and in between. Sometimes, as many as fifteen people would be standing along the walls of The Spot to read, eat, and some even to buy the hundreds of weekly publications available.

They had newspapers in English, Yiddish, and even in Polish for people like Miss Triplousky, who immigrated from Poland not too long ago. Considering the size of Woodlake, one might wonder if there were enough people to purchase this array of material, yet Mr. Henkins felt it necessary to have it here. He would switch out the issues weekly and monthly, depending on their publication schedules.

Often getting into The Spot would be very treacherous with stacks of bikes piled high in front of its doorway. Woodlake was easily traveled by bikes, and The Spot was one of the favorite locations for kids to rid themselves of their weekly allowances. The Spot was a magnet for kids because each week the newest comics were displayed on its racks, and every candy was ready for the taking. There were little toys as well; pink Spud bouncing balls, jump ropes, and sets of jacks.

When the kids were away in school, folks would stop by on their way to work to buy the daily news, and gossip.

Teens loved it as well, for there were rows upon rows of the latest movie and teen publications. There were magazines where they could sing along with the words of any popular hit from American Bandstand, and others that had covers which told which teen idols were dating who. They could buy any possible gum- bubble or spearmint, and maybe run into friends hanging out peering through the many racks as they leafed through the pages. Teen Life, 16 Magazine, Teen Screen, and the nefarious True Confessions were but a few.

Mr. Henkins secretly wished the children who frequented The Spot would purchase their treats and be gone. After locking up each evening, there were candy wrappers everywhere and sticky fingerprints on the walls. He'd wash off the smudges, but soon after, they'd reappear. It made his life difficult. He could not find a solution. After all, these children were the beloved urchins of their parents, and weren't going away. He also understood they were his customers.

Mrs. Henkins used to take charge of the children. It had always been his wife's job as the tiny ones on tip toes pointed to the penny candies in the jars lining the counter asking for jelly bellies or licorice sticks. She'd help them reach for the Little LuLu comics if their tiny arms couldn't get them down.

Sadly, her recent illness left Mr. Henkins in charge. They were a team. They were partners for life. Mrs. Henkins was always by his side. Mrs. Henkins had tried for months to carry on as usual, but fatigue from her daily treatments made her too weak to continue. She encouraged him to continue working in the Spot. She understood that if he sat all day watching her weaken, he would shortly follow. So, begrudgingly, here he was, in charge of everyone and everything.

"Hey, Mr. Henkins can you help me with this zipper, it's stuck," Little Joey shouted from the bathroom. Mr. Henkins couldn't believe his ears. Wasn't it enough that he picked up after them every day? Wasn't it enough that these unruly kids seemed to have no appreciation of his property, and now he had to assist one in his own store bathroom? He pretended not to hear. Joey was seven, how could he not open his own zipper? Mr. Henkins continued reading the Woodlake high school football scores, when again Joey screeched out; this time so much louder, "Mr. Henkins help, help!!!." " Darn you, Joey. Where's your mother?" Mr. Henkins mumbled to himself. He looked around and waited for someone else to go to the little boy's rescue, but no one seemed to have heard, or perhaps they purposely tuned him out. Mr. Henkins shook his head in disgust and reluctantly walked towards the bathroom.

As he peered in, there was Joey on the floor with his red checkered shirt tail somehow wedged in the rungs of his zipper, his brown suspenders were twisted around his arms. His blond wispy hair flopping over his tearful eyes and he was lying on his back, with his feet propped against the wall, as he struggled to get his pants up. Mr. Henkins wanted to yell at the boy, but laughter came tumbling out of his mouth. "How did you manage to do that Joey?" he chuckled.

He carefully lifted Joey onto the toilet seat, quickly untangled his zipper, and suspenders as Joey sprung up like a grasshopper. Joey, in tears at this point, grabbed a hold of Mr. Henkins and couldn't stop hugging him. "I love you Mr. Henkins, you're the best!"

"Oh, stop this nonsense," said Mr. Henkins, gently picking him up after freeing him from his predicament. He carried Little Joey to the front of the store and soothed him with a large lollipop. "Now Joey, stop that crying, you are a big boy." Joey sniffed a little, rubbed his nose on Mr. Henkins' shirt, hugged him again and left as Mr. Henkins watched him find his mother who hadn't noticed that he had been missing.

Next, Mr. Henkins rapidly turned to the cacophony of squirming children leaning against the walls of The Spot. and bellowed in his booming voice, "How many times must I tell you if you aren't buying anything, GET OUT, GET OUT! NOW!!!". As everyone momentarily faced him, the children snapping to attention, he flapped his hands in the air and signaled towards the door for everyone to exit.

In an instant everyone did an about face, ignoring his orders, and returned to what they were doing.

No one left.

Mr. Henkins frustrated and annoyed, threw up his hands, turned and finished reading his newspaper.

Chapter 25

Toby's Home Economics 101

"Walked to school, had a history test, worked on the green organza apron in Home Ec., and walked home…, I would love to burn that apron!" that was an entry from Toby's secret diary that she kept locked with a key under her bed.

Lots of kids from the three schools in Woodlake frequented Bob's diner. Toby Lester often would stop by after school and sit at the counter to have a chocolate shake, her favorite. Looking forward to anything but school was heavenly for her.

"Boring, oh so boring," was Toby's response to her time spent at Woodlake's Junior High.

Small town life was not the script she fantasized for her life. Those rare trips when her mother took her into New York City, only an hour and a half from Woodlake, was the life she yearned for herself. Skyscrapers towering to the heavens, people packed together in humongous crowds, and the culmination sitting silently in the cavernous Radio City Music Hall seeing the Rockettes, wearing sparkling outfits, tapping in perfect formation across the stage- that was the story of her life she would write one day.

"Certainly, for some in Woodlake, all things were fine, but not for me," Toby sighed. Try as she might she was forever late to class. She would get warnings from the hall monitors, and then sit in detention on a routine basis due to her oversights. Detention, a place where over active kids were sent to, to quiet down, and stifle their creative selves, Toby again pined.

She never understood why it was of such importance to get to homeroom and listen to the same repetitive announcements that she had been hearing for the past eight years of her public-school life.

Over the loudspeaker, "Please stand for the Star-Spangled Banner, repeat the pledge of allegiance. Our morning prayer will be Psalm 23. Bologna sandwiches and macaroni are available in the cafeteria today, along with tomato soup. Choir auditions will be held after school."

"I can't believe tomato soup again," Toby whispered loudly to her friend behind her. Just then, as if the assistant principal could hear her, Toby thought, "No talking during morning announcements!" the loudspeaker continued.

She enjoyed the walks to school, and the walks home, but the time in school seemed a huge waste of her time. She was trying to become an entrepreneur by selling greeting cards door to door in her neighborhood. She noticed on the back of her Little Lulu Comics it touted that if she could sell fifty dollars worth of greeting cards, she could win a teacup Chihuahua or at least be eligible for the drawing to win one. She knew it might take a while since she had only sold three boxes so far, but she was hopeful that things would be picking up before too long.

Today was the most dreaded class she attended- Home Economics 101. One of the required assignments was to complete an apron. She just couldn't understand why it was so important to have the seams of her green organza apron so perfectly aligned. It was five months of basting and rebasting the seams and yet no end in sight. It was just a square piece of organza with two long sash pieces to tie around her waist. Miss White was never, ever was satisfied with it. The stitches were crooked, the sash was uneven, the waist band was lopsided, and on and on Miss White found fault. Toby was going to be an actress or a reporter; not someone who wore organza aprons and served guests pate hors- d'oeuvres at fancy dinner parties.

"Just do as your teacher's say in school," Toby's father declared with his prideful chuckle. "Getting a C is perfection! C stands for Courage, Capable, and Curious. After all, your mom and I could care less. Us Lesters have always been free thinkers. Just pass the class and move on!" Her mother never pushed for more than that, either. "Toby, you know I never cared for sewing or cooking. Your dad, on the other hand, loves those sorts of things. We both just want you to be happy." Toby was able to eke through her academic offerings but wondered if her parents truly understood how unbearable this Home Ec. Class had become. It was quite possible, Toby began believing, "I won't graduate due to receiving Fs for my less than perfect dumb, ugly apron."

The tuna casserole lesson, that lasted over three weeks, made Toby weep daily. Tuna had been Toby's favorite up to then, but when raisins and cottage cheese were brought into the mix, it became intolerable. The taste was downright awful!

"This, ladies, is how you can make a delicious spread to serve your gentlemen callers," Miss White emphasized.

"Gentlemen Callers," was a phrase that Toby had only heard in Gone with The Wind. Toby's mother never spoke of gentlemen callers, and the word was that Miss White never had any callers of any kind herself. Miss White, who was close to sixty, had always lived with her younger feeble-minded sister, who was close to fifty.

Toby would have rather been allowed to take wood craft like the boys, but that was out of the question at Woodlake Junior High. Girls took Home Ec. and the boys got Shop. She had heard from her father that men were the most famous chefs in the world, but that didn't matter at Woodlake Junior High. Choice was not an option. In fact, at Bob's there were never any females in the kitchen nor men serving food.

Like clockwork, every week on Thursday at one o'clock, all the seventh-grade girls were scheduled to march over to the free-standing house across from the school to have Miss White turn each one of them into perfect ladies. "I can't believe that here we are again," Toby chatted to her friend, "I suppose no one will listen to what we want until we're grown up and I hope that happens really, really soon!"

The home ec. house was painted white with carved lattice work trimming the door. Two flower boxes, attached to the front windows, were usually overflowing with petunias, or tulips. It was magical from the outside but was a prison for Toby with no chance of escaping.

Miss White even taught them about the dos and don'ts of menstruation, blushing all the way through the lesson. "Girls, you must pin your napkins neatly to your sanitary belts and dispose of them by wrapping toilet paper tightly three times around each napkin until you can bounce it into the garbage can without it ever opening." "Why is this necessary?" Toby demanded to know. Several girls giggled.

"Enough, ladies! Toby, I don't want to hear another word

from you. Do you understand? We cannot have visitors entering our restrooms and see unkempt napkins strewn all over the place. Do you?"

"No, Miss White," as Toby rolled her eyes.

Toby was always self-conscious walking to class with a wet napkin pinned onto her underwear during her period days. It was only a few months ago while walking to English class that her panties became wet. She rushed into the nearest bathroom and was shocked to see red flowing into the toilet. Not knowing who to tell, she put wads of toilet paper between her legs to keep from soiling her dress. Walking back to class she felt like a large goose waddling through the hallways. She knew everyone could tell something was wrong. She wanted to tell her teacher, but Mr. Wright was a man, after all!

Toby along with the other girls had to practice rolling the toilet paper around each Kotex napkin, and one by one toss it into the receptacle. As if it wasn't bad enough attending the Home Ec. Class, this display of foolery was beyond embarrassing. Toby thought for sure she would be doomed to stay in Junior High forever because her napkin tossing and toilet paper wrapping skills were never up to par.

Soon, June would be approaching, and summer vacation after that. It wasn't coming fast enough. As Toby dragged herself to Woodlake Junior High, she realized that this was the last week to complete her green organza apron. It was the seventh month of working on this project and she was beginning to feel that perhaps she should have begged her mother to assist her in its completion. She wanted to end this year and go on to eighth grade with her friends, but up to now it wasn't looking too promising. She clutched the apron in her hand and knew today was the day.

"Miss Lester!" Miss White shouted out last week as Toby was about to scurry down the steps, "Please step into my office. Miss Lester, I know you are aware that I am still not satisfied with your apron. If we are to go out into the world, we must know how to sew evenly and cook with ease. Your tuna casserole I will say is passable, but that apron?" "Yes, Miss White, I know I have been trying, and next week I think you will be pleased," Toby said without believing a word she had spoken.

Lunch was over, and Toby and her friends crossed the street to their Home Ec. class. Next week, if Toby passed, she would be assisting with her classroom clean up, taking down the bulletin boards, helping to check in the textbooks, and attending the end of year assemblies. She entered the Home Ec. building and placed the apron on Miss White's desk in the back corner. Miss White showed the ladies a special film on kitchen cleanliness. As the projector hummed, Toby saw Miss White go to her desk and inspect her apron. She seemed to be turning it over and over, again and again. The lights were flicked on, and finally, Miss White served brunch and cookies as an end of project treat. As they got up to go, Miss White pulled Toby aside.

"It isn't the best apron I've seen in my career, but I think you squeezed out a C-," she whispered. There wasn't more Toby could say, but "Really, Miss White? I passed, really? Thanks!" Toby knew, next school year, it would start all over again. She already heard it would be an uglier cooking hat, which was always the girls eighth grade's project.

For now, Toby thought, it would be months, and that seemed a long time away.

Soon would be summer vacation. Summer vacation meant no more school and even better no more sewing, at least for the time being.

Chapter 26

My Beautyberries Never Looked That Good

ary would always join the Girls on Fridays at Bob's, but her greatest passion was being out in her garden. Her beloved Wen left her alone after fighting his illness for years. It wasn't as she had originally mapped out her life. She thought she would grow old with Wen, travel, and enjoy many hours in her beloved garden together.

Five years had passed, and after searching and praying for someone to fill his void, she had resolved herself to finding serenity alone in her beautiful garden. She'd found contentment also, spending quality time with her close friends.

Woodlake was a fanciful place for Mary. It had glorious tall pines and cool winters which allowed for a ravenous display of flowers to bloom in the spring and summer months. Mary loved to take long walks around the lake that Woodlake was named for. She would stop at each turn to explore and examine every passing twig or tiny sprouts on its pathways.

Nature could fill the void left by the passing of her husband. When her dear Wen died, she would spend many solidary hours in her garden to bond with her beloved trees and flowers. The smell of the earth and seeing the tiny droplets hanging on to the fusion of leaves, bonded by the early morning dew upon the majestic weeping willow trees, made some of her loneliness dissipate. It was a safe haven, a place to reflect and have no one sorrowfully pitying her. Mary refused to be pitied. The surroundings of Mother Earth never judged her but engulfed her into its arms; accepting her exactly as she was.

It was on one such spring day, that Mary got terribly agitated. This was a rarity for Mary. She hardly ever got agitated. It was quite uncharacteristic of her.

While looking out her picture window into her back yard, she saw that right between her perfectly positioned black walnut and large American chestnut, were growing clumps of beautyberries. Those bright red berries, attached to stiff green stalks couldn't have been in such an unlikely location. Mary knew every inch of her carefully positioned garden, and she would remember if in fact they were planted in that particular spot. She loved and allowed for the randomness of nature, yet this Beautyberry placement gnawed at her.

It was several months ago at the Armory in Brickshire Township, that Mary had persuaded the "Girls" to attend the annual New Jersey Plant and Flower Extravaganza. Mary was never too demanding, in fact she never demanded anything, yet, she had insisted that everyone must attend this event. Irene could kill a plant with a stare, and Shirley only knew two classifications of flora- roses and daisies, but the fact that Mary demanded this one thing made them jump to the occasion. Mary crossed each day off her kitchen calendar, awaiting the arrival of this event. It just couldn't be missed.

At precisely nine o'clock, Irene and Shirley waited outside Bob's as Mary carefully drove up in her large, oversized blue Cadillac. They had managed to have a quick breakfast and wouldn't dare disappoint Mary. It was almost an hour to the Armory and Mary wanted to be the first to arrive before it opened. The drive to Brickshire Township was glorious. The tall Jersey pines led the way and the Girls chatted about their week.

"I heard that Lillian took Carmela to the movies. Wasn't she that young girl who was sent off away to have her baby?" "No, one knows for sure, but it seems the only logical thing?" Mary tuned out. If nothing else, this would be an adventure to leave the safety of Woodlake, and escape for an afternoon with good friends. It was her yearly pilgrimage that energized her with tranquility and joy.

As the blue Cadillac approached the converted armory, Mary valeted her car and almost jumped out as they arrived. Inside there were rows of vendors from every Jersey County and some that had come from other states. Vendors were selling fruit trees, and others specializing in tulips. Men were demonstrating mulching devices, and tables displayed an array of seeds.

Irene and Shirley managed to find the food booths way in the back, as Mary lagged behind overwhelmed by the magnitude of it all. Mary spotted a small booth in the corner of the huge convention-like arena and eyed a table full of green plants with a variety of red and purplish berries. They drew her in. She became transfixed with their simplicity.

"Can I answer any questions?" a young woman behind the

table in a gauze pleaded skirt, and ruffled curly hair tied with a red paisley bandana had asked Mary.

Mary was so engrossed in the specialness of the berries that she didn't hear the question at first. When Mary got drawn into these moments of discovery, everything got tuned out. At last she mumbled, as if in a trance, "My Beautyberry plants never looked that good." "Oh, thanks. The ones we grow are some of New Jerseys finest specimens. Are you giving them too much water?" the young woman inquired. "They need the right amount. Not too much and not too little….," she continued.

Mary had to think a moment. For Mary these were never questions to be answered in haste. Planting and growing were extremely serious business.

"Actually, I never thought about that, I think they have always been in my yard, I guess. I mean the berries usually don't have enough time to grow due to those pesky birds and squirrels. Don't get me wrong I love those creatures, but it is a constant battle," Mary went on.

She had hundreds of plants to consider, but somehow at this moment those beautyberries were causing her tremendous unrest. But, before Mary could decide if in fact she had been giving them too much water, Shirley and Irene came back down the aisle asking when they could sit down for lunch. Mary wanted to continue the conversation, but when Shirley and Irene wanted to eat, she wouldn't stand a chance. For a second, Mary glanced over at the glorious beautyberries on the table and knew she'd have to get her answer, of too much or too little water, another time. Disappointed she quickly asked, "Sorry, I do want to know, do you have a card? You have been so kind and perhaps we can chat about my beloved beautyberries another time." Mary was able to switch gears and got into the Girls joy of picking delicacies to indulge in.

There were many foods that the Brickshire Ladies Auxiliary had prepared. Along with the floral booths and gardening items, there was always places for people to sit and relax after marching up and down rows of plants along with hundreds of indoor and outdoor items.

There were food choices for every palate. The fluffy tuna sandwiches with apple slices, or the bright orange carrot cakes Shirley and Irene couldn't pass up. Then there was the tasty freshly squeezed orange juice. Even Jersey's pumpkin pies. Shirley and Irene loved eating as much as Mary enjoyed planting. Mary certainly wasn't opposed to those choices either. She loved her friends.

After sitting at one of the folding tables with carefully arranged sandwiches and completing the meal with iced tea it was eventually, time to leave. They had stuffed their faces, and the Girls were full. Shirley and Irene were satiated with the tasting of the many homemade delicacies the Ladies Auxiliary had sold at the show, and Mary was full of happiness along with being surrounded by such a vast array of vines and a plethora of plants. Of course, seeing those beautyberries had taken her breath away. She placed the card in a special spot in her purse and would call that young lady soon.

Now, starring out of her backyard window, Mary had wondered if she had waited, and gotten the full answer at the plant and flower show, perhaps this wouldn't be happening. She tried to remember exactly how she planted those beautyberries. Just last week she had been summoned by the town's invasive plant inspector. As she arrived home after church, Buzz Caldwell turned up in his battered truck.

"Mary, as I was passing by your house, I saw those yam-leaved clematis. Those ravaging invasive vines are protruding out over your garage and tumbling down into your backyard. I will take care of it now!" Before she could answer, he had proceeded to take out his pickax and chop it away, while Mary, in her large blue hat with the fake white gardenias, bent over on the ground taking care that her beautyberries weren't damaged. Her shoes got slightly soiled, but triumphantly she protected them.

"Buzz you be careful now, those yam-leaved clematis are pretty tricky to get out. You know their root system goes on for days." Buzz kept chipping away and eventually pulled every last piece of its damaging roots. After, Mary went into the house to get Buzz a large glass of ice water, he drove off, and she was again able to refocus on her beautyberries.

Again, she thought, how did they manage to be growing between her treasured nut trees? Perhaps these were not put there by her? She was always meticulous over her plant's placement. The plants had to be arranged into exact areas in which they would flourish best.

She looked at those beautyberries again and was convinced she wouldn't have wanted them in that particular spot. No sun, too much shade. Yet, as she opened her back door, there they were, and not as she had seen them at the show. Mary starred at her dull, dark, almost burgundy berries hanging, sagging onto their stalks. She kept trying to figure it all out but couldn't. Should she keep them there or find another spot?

As she kneeled in the warm, wet grass groping for her spade and clippers, suddenly she became less agitated. Under her was the soft groundcover she had chosen last year. The oddly named bloodroots, almost twinkled in the sunlight coming through the trees. Under her feet, the curled leaves began to open. Her mind began to drift to Buzz. Could he have been the one to place the yam-leaved clematis near her garage? No, he wasn't such a man. As hard as she thought she couldn't remember how those beautyberries were in that spot between the trees.

Suddenly, Mary watched the butterflies quietly light on the ruby ground cover. She recalled the card the young woman had given her at the flower show. She could call her and ask her for the answer as to why the beautyberries weren't flourishing.

While these thoughts were in her head, an epiphany occurred to her, these flowers and herself weren't flourishing as they should. It all was becoming clearer to Mary.

"Solitude is important, but being with friends, is equally important. I will always have a place in my heart for Wen, but those beautyberries, like myself, must find space, perhaps for others or someone in particular," Mary told herself. "It isn't so much that my beautyberries are beginning to wither, but perhaps I am too," Mary finally understood.

Who, or when this would happen she didn't know, but she was opening and willing to finally explore those possibilities.

Those none-too-perfect beautyberries would have to do for the moment. She understood that this life of hers was not as she had planned or hoped for, and perhaps in time she would decide the fate of her none too perfect beautyberries.

Buzz had left his number in case she might need his services again. She had tacked up his business card near the phone, next to the woman's business card from the flower show. Maybe one of them would have her answers?

Mary laughed to herself and knew the answer to her beautyberry quandary would have to wait, at least for the moment. She got up, almost skipped to the house, opened the backdoor, pulled one of the business cards off the wall, reached for the phone, and dialed Buzz's number first. He probably was about her age, she giggled again to herself. She had overheard at Bob's Diner that he too was single. With a huge smile she held onto to the phone and waited for Buzz to answer.

Chapter 27

Nathan's Time Factor

Nathan Twitters just couldn't understand why 10 o'clock didn't mean 10 o'clock. His mom never arrived anywhere on time. As a little boy, he always waited on the steps of his grade school, watching all the children leaving as he sat for what seemed like forever. Mothers would stop, seeing him sitting and staring at the ground and ask, "Are you alright Nathan, do you need a ride?" "No, thank you," he apologetically whispered wishing that for one day he could switch places with anyone and not be the boy always left behind. One day he had sat for almost two hours when his mom arrived in her oversized pink rollers, secured with a paisley scarf. His mom was excited about recently purchasing a new recliner for their living room and didn't even apologize for leaving him there scared and alone. Nathan's anxiety had turned to fear thinking that maybe this time he had been forgotten.

As a teenager he was always first out the door in the

mornings. His mother never had to force him out of bed. As an adult, he had high expectations of others being on time. Being hyper punctual, he had to learn to be accepting of others who time meant little, but it was never easy for Nathan.

When he became a teacher, he always stood at the high school's gate before the principal arrived, and would always think, "why isn't he here on time". In fact, he was here at least forty minutes before everyone else, everyone else except for Nathan, who was there an hour before. Nathan stood at his classroom door watching each student enter, making mental notations of who was in first, and those who straggled behind. It was a habit he couldn't break. All those years ago of being left on the steps of his elementary school had ingrained this habit into his DNA.

Rosaline, (his love and in Nathan's dreams, soon to be wife), was aware of Nathan's affinity to time, and loved him despite his extreme punctuality. She arrived at the diner on time and was ready for her customers, for she knew that to be a good waitress, her job was to make her customers happy.

Out of the diner was another thing, and she worried less about time and more about her surroundings. Rosaline rocked from side to side with her limp as she stopped to look at the children in the playground, or tiny critters rushing up a tree. If she missed the beginning of a movie at the Strand, it was of little importance to her. Life as a child was very difficult for her and now, she took control of each moment and did as she pleased.

Nathan and Rosaline were good together. He spoke little and she spoke a lot. He was punctual and she not so much. They were two incomplete halves, that fit and formed a whole. Nathan Twitters and Rosaline ambled down the streets of Woodlake on a quiet Sunday evening when he thought he heard thunder in the distance.

"Rosaline, did you hear that? I guess we better get to the Strand before we are soaked. I didn't bring the umbrellas, did you," he asked her.

Rosaline loved the rain, the sun, the snow, all changes in the seasons. It made the day a little more special. A little more different. She was picked on as a child, so she shied away from being outdoors unless absolutely necessary. As an adult, she learned to embrace her quirkiness and if anyone happened to stare in her direction she might respond with a big smile or stare them down, depending on her mood.

What she loved about Nathan Twitters was his quiet introversion. His silence allowed her space to be. Rosaline had space to talk about whatever she desired, or at other times for them to walk in silence and just be. A perfect match.

"Rosaline, the movie starts in ten minutes, we have to buy tickets, get popcorn, and find our seats." he persisted. Being late wasn't an option, especially for a movie. The thought of not being on time was making Nathan quake. "Please, Rosaline, hurry!"

As they were about to cross the street, Nathan quickly reached for Rosaline and pulled her back, because rounding the corner was Mr. Bing, Woodlake High School's band teacher, and one hundred and fifty members of his award-winning marching band that played every football game on Woodlake's football field.

Apparently, Mr. Bing found out that the River Township's band was planning a huge half-time show, and he thought one more practice for Woodlake was what was needed to let them and everyone else know who in fact was the best. Normally, he would have practiced on the high school field, but the little league had borrowed it due to another flood on their field.

First around the bend, came the drum majorette with his long-pointed stick going up and down setting the tempo for the players. He strutted and moved his knees in high flinging kicks. Nathan wanted to squeeze between him and the band, but majorettes behind were flinging their batons high into the air and he was afraid that Rosaline might get hit. As if that wasn't enough, he thought, flag and gun twirlers fell in behind and flipped their flags and guns in every which direction. Nathan realized that if they didn't act quickly, the movie was going to start and start without them. Rosaline got caught up in the pageantry and almost forgot where she and Nathan were headed.

"Rosaline on the count of three let's get going when the flags pass us. Now!" he demanded. All this was becoming too much commotion for him. He had checked and rechecked the Strand's timetable and knew to the minute when the movie was to begin. If they didn't cross now, he would miss the opening credits, and that was not acceptable.

Just then, he was startled when he heard a loud whistle blow from Mr. Bing who had been following along the easement of the street. With that, the trumpets blasted out an earsplitting cacophony of the beginning notes of the Star-Spangled Banner. Cars were backing up, and other bystanders meandering along the sidewalks took off their hats to salute. As the instruments finally fell into harmony Rosaline grabbed Nathan's hand and suddenly all the tension drained out of his body.

As the marchers passed them by, the trombones guttural slides slid back and forth, French horns heralded the day, flutes twinkled, and the kettle drum thunderously rolled down the street. As the cymbal player was crashing his large shiny discs against one another, Nathan put his hand over his heart, yet not letting go of Rosaline, as he squeezed her hand even tighter.

For a flash of a second, out of habit, he checked his watch, but he finally knew that time would just have to wait. There would always be another movie, but never a moment such as this.

Chapter 28

Toby Strikes Out

One good quality Toby clung to, was her ability to emote and catch the attention of her Drama club sponsor, Mrs. Asher. Every April, a week before the Woodlake's Junior High School let out for Spring recess, a huge pageant was held. It was going to take place tomorrow evening in the auditorium. The Woodlake's Junior High choir sang, Mrs. Triplousky's dance group performed, the drama club did a short play, along with children who were chosen to read poems they memorized for months. The auditorium was decorated with large paper flowers in pinks and yellows constructed by the elementary children, and crepe paper streamers were hung upon the walls and doorways. It was often difficult for the children to contain their enthusiasm as the days up to Spring recess approached.

"Boys, and Girls," Mrs. Asher bellowed, "please calm down as we listen to Toby read the famous poem by Ernest Lawrence Thayer, Casey at the Bat." There were daily rehearsals during lunch time. The children filed in and were supposed to eat quietly until it was their turn to advance to the stage. Mrs. Asher felt it was a good way to contain everyone, and get the performers used to being in front of a large audience.

Toby approached the microphone, and began, "The outlook wasn't brilliant for the Mudville nine that day; The score stood four to two, with but one inning more to play."

Mrs. Asher gave a stern look across the cavernous room, atop the cacophony of wooden seats squeaking, before the children finally quieted down. Toby had put to memory most of this literary poem. She obviously wasn't a baseball fan. In fact, she had hoped that Mrs. Asher had given her the Walt Whitman piece to read, but Mrs. Asher felt this poem displayed more of Toby's excellent reading talents. Toby rarely stumbled over the somewhat difficult vocabulary for a twelve-year-old. Her father, a frustrated actor, gave her many elocution lessons.

Toby continued, "Ten thousand eyes were on him as he rubbed his hands with dirt; Five thousand tongues applauded when he wiped them on his shirt." As each phrase dropped from her lips, she got more animated and the children began to fixate on Toby's broad movements, as she pantomimed Casey curling his lip before batting.

Suddenly, the lunch bell sounded, and noise erupted as the students scrambled out the large swinging doors to their classes. Toby felt pride in having the ability to get everyone's attention; as she heard Mrs. Asher yell out, "Good job today, Toby. You're ready," Toby hurriedly left to her math class. Her math class was sheer torture. She stared at the clock until it was finally time for school to end.

Her mom was usually waiting at the front of the school to walk Toby home, but today both her mom and dad arrived in her father's Pink Plymouth.

"How was your day? Hop in. Remember you have your dentist appointment." "Dentist appointment, what? Now?"

Toby wanted to be anywhere but in the dentist's office. Even her math class would be better than this dreaded visit. Last month's visit the dentist had discussed Toby's finger sucking.

After months of secretly hiding her nighttime finger sucking from her parents, the dentist confidentially mentioned to Toby, "If you're not going to stop that unfortunate habit, I'll have to put metal prongs in your mouth to force you from pushing your teeth anymore forward than they already are. You don't want to look like Bugs Bunny, do you?"

Bugs Bunny was not at all what she aspired to, but try as she may, when her bedroom lights went out, her finger became wedged in her mouth as she fell off to sleep.

"Toby, glad to see you here today," The dentist said, as she uncomfortably hoisted herself onto the large brown dental chair. The dentist adjusted the flat overhead light and began probing into her mouth. Toby didn't want to hear his next words.

"Well, tell me about our discussion last time you were here. Have you stopped?" Toby so wanted to lie at this moment, but seeing her parents' confusion, Dr. Morgan , hadn't shared their private talk, she solemnly spoke, "I tried, I tried, but couldn't stop." Dr. Morgan knew he had no choice but to tell Toby's parents that an immediate intervention had to be done, or he wouldn't be able to correct their daughter's protruding teeth.

"Today, is the day. You've given me no choice." Three metal prongs, on a wire, were hung in the back of Toby's large front teeth. By placing them there eventually the pricks to her thumb would stop the habit.

"They'll be uncomfortable for a few days, you'll get used to them, and in about a month or so I'll remove them. It's for your own good." The next morning, Toby was waiting outside Mrs. Asher's office before anyone arrived. "Please, Mrs. Asher I won't be able to do my poem tonight. I can't get up in front of everyone and be lisping. It's too embarrassing. The children will laugh at me."

"No excuses, you must go on. Your name's in the program, and you're one of the best in my class. As I've taught you, the show must go on, young lady." With those ominous words, it was apparent to Toby that she'd have to perform, and her life as she knew it was over. Toby was next after Mrs. Polinsky's dance troop. As Toby approached the microphone, her throat became dry as she unwillingly began her oration.

All was going ok and then the words, "A thickly theighlence" fell upon the patrons of the game. The poem's namesake closely followed. "They thought if only Kay thee", low titters rose from the children and a few parents. As she approached each line her elegantly "Kay thee", mighty Kay thee," created louder chuckles from the crowd.

At last, almost in tears, one could barely hear Toby utter the final lines of the famous poem, "And somewhere men are laughing, and somewhere children shout, but there is no joy in Mudville—mighty Kay thee hath struck out."

Chapter 29

Yellow Polka Dot Bikini Contest

Rosaline liked working in Bob's Diner. She never questioned if there were other jobs or other professions that she might pursue. This was her home and her family. During her high school days, at first, she would come by after school to bus the tables, next to assist Ginger the other waitress, and now she was a full-fledged waitress, with her own station and bunches of regulars.

When she was a freshman in high school, she thought of becoming a secretary, but, after her endless struggles with typing, she knew the diner was the place for her. She felt very important within these walls and rarely had to confront those awful bullies. Once, when she was eating her lunch in the school cafeteria, a group of girls made oinking noises in her direction.

They would whisper as they passed her in the halls, "Hey, big butt, oink oink." She wanted to drop out of school so many times, but the small quiet voice in her head kept reminding her that the people in Bob's Diner wanted her, and that she wasn't going to give up! She always managed to maintain her positive outlook in the face of adversity.

It was true she thought, "I do need to lose weight, I should exercise more, and stop eating all those wonderful desserts that were always available at Bob's." She tried walking more and doing jumping jacks, but after five minutes of huffing and puffing she would give up. Her mom was quite obese and would lecture Rosaline about the virtues of being thin and eating properly-- here was her mother who was way over two-hundred- and thirty-pounds giving Rosaline advice. She had wondered what it would be like to go on a date or be invited to school dances, yet the food talked much louder to her than her will power.

At Bob's in her bright yellow waitress uniform and space shoes, she was left alone, as long she didn't mess up anyone's order. Sometimes, one of the freshmen boys would try to cop a feel by hugging her and getting pressed deep into her huge breasts, but they never meant any harm.

Summer was coming and Rosaline knew the seasons were changing because the high school girls would come into the diner with red cheeks and blotchy skin from sitting in their interweaved webbed lawn chairs way too long during the afternoon sun. They had crisscrossed patterns imprinted on the backs of their legs which was a dead giveaway. Getting the perfect Jersey tan was high on their priority list. The girls would cram into a booth, maybe six or more at a time, collapse and ask for large chocolate shakes. Rosaline often wondered how they kept their tiny figures when they lived on shakes and fries all summer long.

On one hot July day, she overheard the girls talking about a yellow polka dot bikini challenge. Apparently, in the nearby department store window, a mannequin recently displayed an outlandish yellow polka dot bikini, perhaps fashioned after the Billboards chart number one song; which sold over one million copies. The female mannequin had a yellow polka dotted flowered sarong draped over its torso and the top, although quite skimpy, at least covered most of its female anatomy. The girls giggled and said they were going to try and trick Beth into buying it and joining them on their foray to the Jersey shore. They couldn't wait for her to embarrass herself at the beach. "It would be the funniest thing to see her wear that ugly, outlandish suit", Ronnie babbled on.

Rosaline knew Beth because she often worked in the diner's kitchen washing dishes on weekends. Beth was a rather shy girl, very polite, and a hard worker. She didn't speak too often to the young girl, but she could see that a new set of those unkind creatures were concocting a way to belittle Beth by fostering their friendship upon her. Memories of her own childhood came rushing back. Rosaline knew at that moment, she didn't know how, that she would help Beth get the revenge that she was never able to get herself, those many years ago.

Rosaline found it hard to believe that it was getting close to twenty years since she graduated high school and girls were still as spiteful as they had ever been. When they came into the diner they were always very polite and respectful, but this type of hateful pettiness was usually done when no one was around. Walking down empty hallways on the way to class, or leaving hurtful notes shoved inside one's locker, that's how their attacks happened. Rosaline wondered how she would assist Beth. She pondered this for many days and even had problems sleeping.

She came into the diner earlier than usual and made it a point to go into the back kitchen where she found Beth sitting at the sink. She was already working on the piles of dishes from the night shift.

"Beth, how has your summer been so far?" Rosaline blurted out. Beth was startled by Rosaline's friendly tone. Usually, Rosaline worked in the front with customers, rarely venturing to the far reaches of the kitchen.

Beth spun around, "Uh, fine I guess, I am happy not to be going to school now." Rosaline tried to carry on the awkward conversation, "Have those girls spoken to you recently? The ones who usually come in here and sit in booth three by the juke box? I think one of them is Ronnie, I'm not quite sure."

Beth, returned to her dishes and then turned back looking straight at Rosaline, "Why do you ask?" Rosaline wanted to say, "Well I want to protect you from the "Yellow Bikini Challenge," but instead she said, "No reason, it seems they were asking about you the other day", she lied.

At that moment Beth swung around again, stood up, and faced Rosaline, "I think you must be mistaken, those girls are bitches, they only say awful things," as tiny droplets of water fell out of her eyes onto her faded apron. What had Rosaline done? Had she overstepped her boundary?

Rosaline didn't know if she should give Beth a hug or leave to return to the front of the diner.

"Beth stop crying! We will get those bitches together, you and I….I don't know how, but together we will figure things out."

Beth again looked into Rosaline's eyes and for some unknown reason, believed her every word. No one ever came to Beth's rescue. In truth no one could have because she kept all this to herself. She had never shared her torment with another human being. She had to believe that this could be her time. She didn't know this woman very well, standing in front of her now. But, maybe this waitress in her bright yellow uniform and space shoes could be her savior.

Rosaline then and there concocted her plan. Step one was a huge billboard constructed in front of Bob's diner announcing the end of summer, Yellow Polka Dot Bikini Contest, just before all the kids returned to school. The lucky winner would win a free burger, fries and a soda for every Friday until Christmas break in December. They would also get their picture on Bob's Wall of Fame for every customer to see as they entered the diner. Perhaps, if they were lucky enough, the contest would drum up enough business for their picture to get into the Woodlake Daily Gazette.

The next step, crazy as it might seem, Rosaline took Beth to Jacob's Department Store the following Sunday, and they bought every single yellow bathing suit in the store. The suits were $9.95, but since summer was coming to an end and only one had sold, Mr. Jacob gave them every last one for fifty percent off. There were twenty in various sizes, and the total was a little over one hundred dollars. Rosaline had savings for a rainy day that she never used and this was the day. They carried them out and placed them into Rosaline's grey 1962 Plymouth. Rosaline drove Beth to the next town over to have a burger and fries. This was step two in their plan, and so far, it was turning out great. A special bond between the ladies was forming and they were loving their secret conspiracy.

Ronnie and the ladies came into the diner, their faces redder than before. The sun was not turning them bronzy, but they still hoped with enough baby lotion lathered everywhere it would happen. They pushed themselves into the booth, and as soon as they settled down, they inquired about the Yellow Polka Dot Bikini Contest.

"Hey, Rosaline, what's this about the contest out front? Yellow Bikini? July? That's about two weeks from now? Can anyone enter?" Ronnie asked with enthusiasm.

Rosaline appearing to be very nonchalant, then said,

"Why sure and there might even be a front-page story in the Woodlake Daily Gazette. It's the first time there has ever been such a contest, and I am sure the whole town will turn out for this," she embellished.

With that, Ronnie and the girls ordered their usual and began chattering about how they would surely be the outstanding beauties of the first Yellow Polka Dot Bikini Contest.

The day for the contest was here, and Rosaline had a lilt to her step. She was happier than normal to serve the breakfast crowd. She was sure no one could compete against Beth, and Beth would at last be the victor. Beth, though, was very apprehensive that perhaps Ronnie had bought that missing thong, and she would again lose another battle. She had tried on the yellow bikini many times secretly in her bedroom, and although she had very small breasts for a fourteen-year-old, her backside was plump, but why had those girls kept saying she was overweight? She had started to believe what the girls told her in private, that she was fat, and would never get a date. In truth her figure was rather like an hourglass. Sadly, when she looked in a mirror, she couldn't see her own beauty.

She had big brown eyes, and very curly brown hair. Her hair would never be long and blond like Ronnie's, but perhaps a boy would like her shiny and wild hair, none the less. Rosaline had taken her to The Spotlight Beauty Parlor to get her nails and toes polished, her eyes tweezed, and her wild curly hair puffed out. Beth looked in the mirror and was starting, even just a little, to believe that she could win this contest.

Sam, the reporter from the Woodlake Daily Gazette, decided to stop by for a cup of coffee and maybe get an interesting story for his Sunday edition. He had read the billboard outside Bob's diner many times driving to work and thought it might make a nice special interest piece to fill things up. He sat at the counter.

It was around 11:00 and Rosaline noted that the contest was to begin in an hour. She didn't see anyone yet, but things always started late on Saturdays. Beth had called that she would be in shortly, and Bob was anticipating extra business, so he had ordered extra pies from the local bakery and cakes for the occasion.

Beth arrived all bundled up and slid in the back entrance. She had her hair pushed back with a bright glittery headband, and matching flip flops. She wasn't sure she would be able to strut around the diner. She wanted to win this contest to show Ronnie and the others that she could do it. On the other hand, she thought, maybe it was better if Ronnie won. After all, maybe this scheme they had planned would never work. She knew that Rosaline was counting on her. She had spent all that money buying all those suits to make sure that Beth had a head start. She couldn't disappoint her.

As the time was getting closer to noon, the diner started filling up. Everyone was curious what was going to happen. The juke box was blasting out tunes, while the crowded diner became packed. The sounds of Lesley Gore belting, "It's My Party," added to the mood. But the lyrics to the inspiration for the contest, "It was an Itsy, Bitsy, Teenie, Weenie, Yellow Polka dot Bikini," got lots of nickels pushed into the juke boxes in Bob's Diner. Ironically, Beth was also shy like the main character in the song's catchy lyrics. "She was afraid to come out of the locker," the first verse reverberated. Many singing along.

This Yellow Polka Dot Bikini Contest was the talk of the town, and everyone wanted to see for themselves what it was all about. Anticipation of what was to come hung in the air. People waited to get in, and others leaned against the counter jostling for a viewing spot. Rosaline and Ginger didn't have a moment to talk. They kept running in the kitchen bringing out eggs, waffles, toast, and coffee-- lots of coffee. Bob stuck his head out a few times looking at all the commotion in his busy diner. Rosaline and Beth kept checking the clock. All waited for Rosaline to announce, "The Contest will begin."

But it was twelve o'clock and none of the girls in Ronnie's pack had shown up. Beth secretly hoped that Rosaline would call it all off. Rosaline didn't know what to do, and Beth was beginning to lose all desire to show off her yellow bikini at this point. How could there be a contest with only one contestant? Time seemed to drag by, and everyone was beginning to wonder if this contest was ever going to take place. Checking the big clock above the entrance door again, it was now almost 12:30, many of the customers had been waiting close to an hour.

Most of them got tired of waiting, and a little annoyed, demanded their checks and left. Beth too, was beginning to get tired. In fact, Beth was hoping that their plot might finally be over. At last, Sam the reporter left too.

The diner was emptying out and the huge build up for the contest had come and gone. Rosaline looked at Beth and began to wonder that perhaps Ronnie and the girls had got the best of them. Beth, too, had the same thought and was angry and sad both at the same time.

She secretly so wanted to come out victorious. She tried not to cry again, and before anyone noticed, or asked too many questions, she rushed into the kitchen, she took off the yellow bikini, quickly changed into her sneakers, jeans, and a t-shirt and started helping out in the kitchen. The dishes were piling up.

The next morning the diner filled up with its normal Sunday morning breakfast crowd. Again, there was a buzz in the diner. People were having their usual breakfast specials of two eggs, toast, bacon, and well-done hash browns, and there were pots of coffee on most tables. Beth had arrived early and was sitting in the back awaiting the first plastic tubs of dirty plates and cups. Rosaline and Gloria were again running all over the place. It seemed strange though.

Today people were not chattering away as they normally did. The Woodlake Sunday edition that Bob kept up front for his patrons was flying off the counter, and everyone had their noses pressed onto the front page. Bob even called the Woodlake office to send over more copies. Rosaline had been running in and out of the kitchen, but suddenly she was forced to stop in her tracks as she was about to deliver one of her pancake platters to Joan, a Sunday regular.

"Roz, take a look at this. Ain't Ronette that girl who always comes into the diner after school?"

"You mean Ronnie, sure, she never showed up for our Yellow Bikini Contest yesterday," Rosaline angrily responded. "What was she thinking! I'm so," and before she completed her sentence, Joan spoke up.

"I think you better read this and SIT DOWN," Joan commanded, as she squished over in the booth to make room for Rosaline.

Rosaline's eyes weren't the best, she squinted some, held the paper at arm's length, and read: WOMAN STRANGLED BY HUSBAND. The Woodlake Daily Gazette headline screamed out across its Sunday edition. Ronette Smith, age 14, came downstairs Saturday morning, while her friends were waiting for her outside in their car, to find her mother dead on her kitchen floor. A yellow bikini bathing suit was wrapped around her throat….it noted.

When September would finally arrive, after summer vacation ended, and Beth began her sophomore year at

Woodlake High she never saw Ronnie again. Ronnie had left, and Ronnie's group of girls never bothered Beth again.

Sometimes as she stepped through the diner's doors, and looked at the faded billboard out front, now covered by new election posters, she wondered where Ronnie might be? How was she doing? What if they had been friends? What if they had strutted through the diner together in their yellow bikinis? Her thoughts were fleeting as she quickly ran into the kitchen.

Bob shouted out to her, "Hey, kid you're late!"

Rosaline called out to Bob, "We need that stew, ASAP," as Beth scurried into the kitchen.

The dirty dishes were piled up as usual, but Beth knew it wasn't ever going to be an ordinary day again. In a melancholy way it was a victory of sorts.

"Beth, hey kid, where the hell are those dishes," Bob yelled out and shattered her thoughts.

"Ok, Bob, hold your horses! Be there in a sec!"

Chapter 30

The Drowning of Abe and George

Buzz, Woodlake's Invasive Plant Inspector, at 6 foot and 160 pounds, was a willow of a man. His unkempt blondish brown hair hung in tendrils across his forehead, and his well-worn baseball cap helped brush some of his locks off his face to allow room for his sparkling blue eyes to greet people with a welcoming glance. Some might say that an Invasive Plant Inspector was an odd job, but without Buzz, the magnificent Jersey pines of Woodlake might have been wiped out years ago. Each encroaching or creeping vine silently wrapping their tentacles around the trunks of these soaring trees, home to birds and bugs alike, were safeguarded from harm by Buzz. These gallant structures would have been ravaged and gone unseen, if Buzz hadn't hacked and chopped those strangling, killer vines out of existence.

As a young boy his greatest past time was climbing up the Woodlake Pine's branches. No tree was too high. Never a dare would he ignore.

"Hey, Buzz, see my kite on that one over there, can you get it for me?" "Hey, Buzz, my cat has climbed up that pine in my back yard and refuses to come down." Before the words were out of their mouths, like Tarzan, Buzz shimmied up each ladderlike branch to bask in the applause from those gazing up from way, way below. Then there were those moments when he would just sit up there watching the tiny people below and swing his legs back and forth. He was born to save these glorious pines. It was his calling.

The Woodlake football team were the fighting Piners. Brown and gold pinecones emblazoned every spectator's shirt, as well as across the huge drum that could be seen and heard as the Piner's band marched up and down the field, prior to each game, to bang out its spirit to the town's supporters.

At each Sunday game, a cry was heard bellowing from within the diaphragms of the exuberant cheer leaders. Wearing brown and white saddle shoes, woolen sweaters, and short flirty skirts, these ladies forever giving strength to the team. The cheer leaders' loud voices harkening the crowd to support the mighty Piners, as if they were protecting each team member and signaling victory.

Buzz never missed a week of writing his letter to the editor of the Woodlake Gazette reminding him that his beloved Woodlake Pines were the town's legacy. After all, the town was named for them. It was the mayor's duty to protect them whenever another home development company tried getting a contract and then plowing down those tall pine trees. Buzz made sure to make his voice heard by presenting his strong point of view at the monthly local town hall meetings. Buzz was steadfast in his fight for saving his beloved trees.

As he approached the lectern to present his argument once again, "I present you exhibit A," pulling out his pointer, displaying his carefully focused shots of the pines circling Woodlake's outer walkways. "You can clearly see our majestic pines reaching to the heavens. Sam, wasn't it there that you asked Ruth to be your wife? Jim didn't you first learn how to fish right next to the bridge under one of those pines?" Buzz had examples for everyone in the basement of the courthouse where the monthly meetings usually took place. All heads nodded as he exhibited why not a twig on those trees should ever be forsaken. When the votes were counted, Buzz usually got his way. His passion made it difficult for anyone to vote against him.

Buzz often would stop off at Bob's Diner for an afternoon snack and to share his day's adventure. For the past two weeks, he had been knee high in mud due to the needed dredging of the town's beloved lake. Lake Carasaljo helped the showcasing of his beloved trees. The woods and the lake gave sanctity to this town. This manmade lake, which had existed for over seventy-five years, had to be drained every ten to twenty years when its waterways stopped moving due to the encroaching roots and leaves clogging the waterways that surrounded it.

Just as the woods were the backdrop to the events of Woodlake's families, if it's lake disappeared its foreground would no longer be available. In every home in Woodlake, there lay a tattered photo album given a prominent spot-on top of every kidney shaped coffee table. At proms, weddings, and high school graduations, families posed tall and proud beneath the pines with Lake Carasaljo glistening behind them. Buzz would do whatever he needed to do to save these hallowed traditions.

"You see it is such a massive job, you wouldn't believe the things we found down there," Buzz spun his tale, "Roger Spank's bike that he somehow drove off the bridge, three wagons from Rob's grocery, a lamp, lots of Coca Cola bottles, and a gold ring with the initials EK. Each day the more we slosh through it all, the more treasures we discover."

As Buzz drank his black coffee and munched on a glazed donut, which Bob had just pulled out of the oven, the usual gang sat and soaked in every word. One would think that there were more interesting topics to be discussed, but Buzz had a way of painting word pictures that had everyone in the diner glued to their seats.

"Does anyone remember that July 4th celebration about two weeks after Charles Weaks died? It was to commemorate Woodlake's 50th anniversary. Its Diamond Jubilee. Maybe ten or fifteen years ago?"

Buzz kept on talking, "The town had purchased two great big presidential cut outs that were supposed to light up. Charlie had gone to the town meeting and had passionately spoken about the need for more patriotism among the youth of Woodlake. He had heard of a man in upstate New York who handcrafted large cut outs of all the presidential figures, and they had red, white and blue lights circling the structures. The lights flashed on and off and spun round and round. Charlie had held his hand across his heart before he saluted the American flag that hung in the meeting room. Yup, as my muddy boots were moving about in the lake, there was Abe and George. Pretty overtaken by vines and gunk, but nevertheless recognizable. I remember that day clearly", Buzz spoke to the mesmerized crowd sitting in the diner.

"All the kids had lined up on the shore with their sparklers in hand, the high school band began to blare out the Star-Spangled Banner, trumpets blasting, tubas grunting, and the mayor picked up a flaming torch to start off the festivities. As he lifted the torch over his head, like the statue of liberty, he tripped over Wally's fire hose, which was there in case one of the sparklers caught fire, right into President Washington's white cardboard wig. Just then, George W. started tumbling into the lake and as it was falling, it bumped into Lincoln's tall stove pipe hat. Next thing you know, the huge presidential cutouts were floating face down in the lake. Mr. Strutter the band director was at a loss for what to do, so he kept swinging his baton. The members of the band lost sight of Mr. Strutter as they watched Abe and George drifting away. Honest Abe and I cannot tell a lie George floated slowly down the lake, to the amazement and awe of the entire town of onlookers, who were overtaken by the commotion along Woodlake's shoreline. No one even noticed Mayor Peeps, who was trying to pick himself up off the muddy ground. And to the disappointment of the Mayor, his magnificent glowing torch had gone out when he had lost his balance and let go of it and watched it fall into the water below. To try and regain a little decorum, Mayor Peeps picked up his megaphone, and got ready to address the crowd; at that exact moment the fireworks started shooting into the sky from a raft in the middle of the lake. Not a single soul listened to anything he had to say.

I heard that he had worked on that speech for over a year in commemoration of the event. There were rockets going off in the distance, as the fires works illuminated the sky. Wow, it was one of the best days of my life. The hot dogs, the sky all lit up. What a day. What a day," Buzz repeated softly, as homage to the event. He looked off into the distance and soaked in the memories.

Bob chuckled to himself from the counter looking out to the gang, soaking in the memories of that day, as well. He recalled every detail as Buzz recounted it. He then broke the silence, "Who wants more donuts? These are on the house."

As the crowd rushed out of their seats, Buzz turned to

Bob with a big grin, grabbed one more of the freshly made donuts and said he had to get back to work. "Till next time!" Before the group had sat down for their second cup of coffee, Buzz was out the door, into his truck. It was his duty and honor to return to his job as caretaker of Lake Carasaljo and its majestic pines.

Chapter 31

Second Chances

The diner was array with the Sunday after church lunch crowd. Rosaline was ambling back and forth to the tables taking and delivering orders and trying to keep up with all the comings and goings of the day.

"What ya having Buzz? How about you Mary?" The clanking of the dishes and the conversations kept the day moving along at a clip.

"Did you hear there was a murder last night?" "Another murder?" "Why I've lived in Woodlake all my life…." "There was Ronnie's mother and now another one!" "Are you sure?"

"I think it was a kid from our own Woodlake High School?"

As Rosaline lurched back and forth across the floor of Bob's Diner, she overheard and tried to piece together what had happened. She wanted to stop and listen to the complete tale, but the over easy eggs and English muffins would be cold if she dared to pause and listen to the complete run down. For the time being, she had to be content in piecing it together.

Graduation for the Woodlake Seniors had happened only six weeks ago and many graduates had been readying themselves to go away to college, saying their good-byes or just letting the summer drift along until they made plans for their futures.

For Bob, Sundays were the busiest and best day of his week. "Over easy, hash browns, no touching," Rosaline screamed leaning over the counter. The frying pans swiftly shook in Bob's skillful hands as he flipped and shook each order in perfect synchronization. "A tall stack with a bacon side. Double hash browns. Burnt." Rosaline and Bob were a well-oiled team. Each plate was arranged to perfection, and never a customer received an order without complete satisfaction.

There was that one time when a bus full of people pulled into the parking lot of Bob's Diner, unannounced. They were on their way to New York City and pulled off the expressway for a quick bite drawn in by the Diner's large flashing sign. It was shortly after the Sunday after church lunch crowd had filtered out. In they walked demanding to be fed quickly. The organizer was heading to the city to bring the group to see an evening performance of Hello Dolly. They had been riding for two or three hours and, for the most part, were grateful to be able to get out of the cramped bus and stretch.

Bob looked up and there were twenty-five hungry customers all wanting to be served at the same time. Under normal circumstances this would have been easy. Usually there was an ebb and flow of people arriving. He sent Rosaline to speak to the organizer and let her know that perhaps a set menu of tuna sandwiches or egg salad with sliced cucumbers and tea and coffee might do the trick. It would be easy to put the slices of bread in rows, spread the tuna and egg concoctions conveyor belt style over each one and be ready before Rosaline served the last cup of coffee. If necessary, he could add a slice of his home-made apple pies that luckily he always had tucked away in his giant refrigerator.

Rosaline asked politely, but it didn't seem to fly. "I don't think everyone will agree on two choices. Couldn't we just order off the menu?" Rosaline didn't know how to respond and ambled back to Bob. He was not happy with the answer, but somehow after an hour of plating everyone's choices, they were off to the city. He always had his "customers first," motto in his head, and wouldn't have been happy if every last customer didn't leave with a smile. Even the ones who he'd probably never see again.

"He was so young. Just eighteen. Just got his diploma. He was robbed at the Texaco- off of Route 12 - and they dumbed his body in the woods. Tragic." Continuing her afternoon routine Rosaline heard snippets of what had happened.

"So what'll it be Beth? Bob are those pancakes ready?" These summer days were flying by as Rosaline embraced each customer's comings and goings. As she danced through the diner, parts of the Woodlake tragedy that was on everyone's lips began to gain some clarity.

"Sherriff Brown found the body this morning as he was combing the area for clues. Heard he thought that maybe the boy had taken off with the robbers. Someone saw him get into the getaway car. Killed. Why?"

As Rosaline heard the bits and pieces she thought back of her days in school. There was that boy who tormented her daily. As she rounded the hallways, he would jump out and pose. Imitating her limp that she had since the fall. "You're so fat, Rosaline. Where're you going Rosaline the Robot? Can't even walk straight." She was the same age as the boy killed when she had thought about dropping out of high school due to her daily bullying. She wouldn't attend her own graduation for fear that she might see the boy who tormented her. She never made that famous graduation march but had the school mail her diploma.

Again, as she balanced the plates, "He was working at the gas station. Night shift. Bashed over the head with a tire iron. They think the killer was a friend of his?" Between the sausage, toast and coffee it was coming together.

So many hours of Rosaline's high school memories were ones of loneliness and taunts. She'd get up in the morning to try and fit in, and there he would be to sneak up behind her and chisel away at any self-confidence she tried to build. "How is it possible that the school would allow an elephant to come inside? You'd never dare tell anyone, who would believe a word you had to say?" Rosaline usually was able to silence his words. Let it all fall behind her. The murder of this high school boy brought it flooding back.

"Hit over the head, and his friend buried him. He confessed right then and there when Sherriff Jones picked him up over in the next county. Kinda' was laughing. The boy had begged to be spared and with one gun shot his life was over."

"Hey, Rosaline got that orange juice?"

"I'm coming, hold your horses."

Rosaline loved this place. She loved these people. She'd find out the name of the boy and send his family a card and include her prayers.

He'd never get a second chance. Luckily, she had.

Lost in thought for a moment Rosaline turned and yelled back to Bob, "Alright I'm walking as fast as I can! This ain't the Olympics."

Chapter 32

Sweet Jersey Moon

L eaves of all colors, red, deep brown, green, orange will be falling from the Jersey trees. As children will be collecting them in between pages of dictionaries, tossed and blown throughout the corners of Woodlake. The Woodlake bus station continuously was transporting people on rides to visit family and friends for the approaching Labor Day Weekend-- the signal that summer was coming to a close. Hundreds of warm humid days turning to cooler ones as fall approached. Backyard blow up pools were being deflated, and school classrooms were readying themselves for the onslaught of new kids rushing through their hallways.

The one last drive to the Jersey shore to watch the seagulls dancing on the sand, the Ferris Wheel spinning, the roller coaster that seemed to be going over the waves, hot corns and grilled steak sandwiches smothered with onions sold on the stands, and people spinning the wheels at the games of chance all along the boardwalk.

It was there that Nathan Twitters found the courage to kneel awkwardly in the sand and ask Rosaline to be his wife. She found it so hard to hobble down the wooden steps leading to the beach, but Nathan insisted.

She found him to be a man of surprises. It was close to midnight; Bob's diner was near to closing. Nathan appeared with a bouquet of red roses demanding that Rosaline grab her sweater and purse and go with him for a drive. Her days of being alone were over, ever since that first kiss six months ago. They had their weekly Thursday night movie and dinner time together. He always walked her home, kissed her goodnight, and waited anxiously for the following Thursday. He knew that he too didn't want any more alone time.

It was Saturday. He was sure she would say yes. He hadn't thought any further than that and decided under the full moon was the right time to ask Rosaline to become part of his life, forever.

Rosaline glanced over at Bob and said she would be in tomorrow morning. After twenty years he could count on Rosaline's word, and smiled as she and Nathan departed the quiet diner. It was unusual for the two to be out together on the weekend, but after six months and years of waiting for someone to need her, she was sure that if Nathan requested her to follow him, then follow him she must. She delighted in the bright red roses, and grasped them tightly in her left hand, while holding tight to her brown purse swinging from her arm.

"You know I am wearing my waitress uniform? I still have my tips in my apron pocket. Are you listening, Nathan? You do know its Saturday, and I have to be back at the diner early tomorrow morning?" She giggled like a schoolgirl, even though her school girl years were long gone.

"Don't worry, I'll have you back before sunrise. I just gotta drive us somewhere before the moon disappears behind those summer clouds."Rosaline kept peering outside and was amazed by the full moon and the soft wind coming through the car's open window. She was somewhat surprised to be riding in a car with Nathan. They always walked on all their dates, and never had left Woodlake together, and definitely never at this hour.

"My mother's car. She hardly ever uses it. I borrow it to take her to church, and shopping, but most of the time it just sits in her driveway. Do you like it? It has air conditioning, but I never use it."

Rosaline had never heard Nathan talk as much as he did tonight. She was drawn to his smile and the excitement.

"Nathan," she hesitated, yet blurted out, "I'd follow you anywhere."

Never in all her life had Rosaline been so forthcoming in her honesty. She couldn't believe that Nathan Twitters, the man who for months had come in the diner ordering toast with butter on both sides, could appear at midnight and she'd follow him anywhere. Just like that.

As they approached the seaside, she began to smell the ocean-- and memories of coming here as a small child with her mother flooded her thoughts. She had stopped coming when the children would tease her because of her awkward gait. Whenever her mother asked why she didn't want to join her, Rosaline always made up an excuse. Yet, here she was with Nathan and all those harsh memories seemed so unimportant.

Nathan parked the car and told Rosaline to wait as he ran around and opened her door, "Leave the roses on the seat, come quickly I don't want that moon to go anywhere, at least not for a little while more. Rosaline hurry!"

Rosaline took Nathan's hand and let him guide her down

the stairs onto the sand. As they reached the shoreline, Nathan dropped to one knee.

"Are you ok, Nathan what's going on?" She had no idea what her sweet Nathan was doing.

"Rosaline, marry me."

Rosaline stared at Nathan and kept staring as he looked up at her. She wasn't exactly sure what she had heard. But, she had heard. She fumbled with her skirt and put her purse down. Tears rolled down her face. She then kneeled too, with great difficulty, and was able to get out the single word, "Yes."

The sand sparkled from the glow above, the Jersey seagulls circled far overhead. Nathan and Rosaline hugged. No diamond ring, no champagne toast, just the sweet Jersey moon smiling down.

Chapter 33

Nathan's Decision

Snow melting at last. Lake Carasaljo's deep green waters glistened once more. Birds and geese gliding on top the water looking for fish, or bread, or anything at all to eat. As always children running along the water's edge to throw rocks, trying to skim them and have them dancing before dropping down onto its murky bottom. Mother's pushing baby carriages, lovers walking hand in hand, an old woman bringing crumbs she had collected over the week to toss to a raft of ducks, and boys searching for toads to capture inside their glass jars or pockets.

Springtime in Woodlake was the realization that the cold was going to subside, and warmth would be returning. Mr. Nathan Twitters couldn't ignore his loneliness anymore and knew it was time to stop ruminating about his life and act.

Summer arrived.

"It was time at last. I've had too many long days alone. Too many long years alone."

"I no longer want to eat alone, watch t.v. alone, and go to bed alone."

For such a man as Mr. Twitters, these were thoughts he had believed were long put to rest, yet upon meeting Rosaline those many months ago, like spring, they were able to bloom from somewhere very deep inside.

He wasn't exactly sure he knew what would lie ahead, but after many long months in thought and contemplation he was ready to be wed to his lovely and adoring Rosaline. He still wasn't too skilled in exchanging words or socializing with others, yet with Rosaline none of that seemed to matter. She was never demanding or pushy. They had now kissed many times and that was at last very comfortable for him, and although she had never spent the night, he was thinking that he might like her to be there when he woke in the mornings.

Rosaline knew that such an odd, unusual man as Mr. Nathan Twitters was going to be The One. He was quirky and different. A man of honor and integrity. When he said he would arrive at five, he meant five and not 5:01. Not having much stability in her life, this was comforting and good for such a woman as Rosaline.

Forever an outsider, forever walking alone, at long last she felt loved and needed. That was more than enough. She had no desires for a grand home or travel. Living in Woodlake among friends and with a good man was the fairy tale she always hoped for, yet, until meeting Mr. Twitters, never seemed a possibility. She wasn't sure when he was going to follow through on his proposal, but it would be soon, of that she was sure. She only had to look down at her finger and twist the small but shiny diamond around and around to know that he had indeed asked her to be his wife. When he had proposed that midnight on the beach there was no ring, but after Rosaline's definitive yes, he had quickly purchased a simple ring to make it official.

After she had said yes, the conversation went no further, for to push Mr. Twitters before he was ready, she learned, was never going to work. He had to process each move and decision, and Rosaline loved him all the same. She had brought up his moving into her house when they married, and after several weeks he agreed that would be an acceptable idea when the time came.

Rosaline began clearing out her closet to allow for Mr. Twitters to have space to hang his clothes, especially his bright red jacket. She made space on her sink for two toothbrushes instead of her singular one. In her heart, she could envision this marriage becoming a reality. So many couples held hands in the diner. So many couples left together. She would be such a couple, too.

Bob and Lilly were anticipating a special diner reception as their wedding gift to the couple, but hadn't gotten too far on the planning. Rosaline had practically grown up in the diner, and they couldn't imagine her and Nathan greeting their guests anywhere else. After all, this was the place where they met and fell in love.

And so it happened.

"Rosaline, let's get married next Sunday," came the words of Mr. Nathan Twitters. "I've been thinking about it long and hard, and summer seems good for us. You invite who you wish. I will ask my mother to walk me down the aisle. Two o'clock? Does that sound good for you?"

Rosaline wasn't expecting it to come so quickly, but she knew if Nathan was ready, so be it. "Sure Nathan, next Sunday sounds perfect. Seven days might be a little quick, but we can do this. Yes, yes," she said as she hugged him and almost spun him around. After waiting for this reality to become true, she couldn't postpone it one more day. "Nathan gotta go, plans to make. Dress to buy, people to invite, I love you Nathan Twitters."

Rosaline became ablaze with activity, "Nathan, you call the church tomorrow and speak to the Reverend. I'll talk to Bob and Lilly about having folks over there after we get married. Is that ok?" "Rosaline, I have to go," Nathan was getting overwhelmed by it all, and he had to gather his thoughts. He never doubted his decision, but it was one of the biggest ones of his lifetime.

"I will be by the diner tomorrow, OK?"

"Sure, Nathan, see you tomorrow."

Rosaline couldn't sleep. She had played this over and over in her head. Church wedding, flowers, organ, friends, and her beloved Nathan by her side. Yes, none of the rest was as important as Nathan, and next Sunday they would be man and wife.

"Keep it all simple," she thought. She knew that Nathan was a quiet person, and although he wouldn't object to any of her plans, simple was the direction she decided would be best for both of them.

Come Monday morning she arrived at the diner almost as early as Bob at 5 AM.

"Gotta talk to you Bob, my wedding, next Sunday." "Hey, let me open the doors first. What, next Sunday!!! Fantastic!"

With that Bob opened the back door of the diner, ran to the phone and dialed, "Hey Lilly, we're going to have a wedding reception in our diner next Sunday, come here as soon as you can! We've got plans to make."

Chapter 34

The Wedding

Sunday arrived and Rosaline and Nathan's wedding day was finally here. It had rained all week in the town of Woodlake, but on Sunday all the clouds left. The sky had its Jersey blue color with bright streaks of white rolling clouds gently dusting the heavens.

Gazing in the mirror and seeing herself for the first time as bride to be, "Mrs. Twitters," Rosaline whispered to herself. She had uttered that name many times. "Nathan Twitters. Groom to be. Alone no more," she continued to whisper.

Rosaline thought briefly of her mother. She had realized long ago that although her mother had raised her, she was never there for her. It had been a struggle to put that part of her life to rest, but at last, thinking about her mother was a distant memory, with no pain attached. She would finally be able to move ahead and start a life bereft of old wounds.

It seemed very quiet in Woodlake this Sunday morning, yet inside Rosaline's home there was much activity. Lilly n' Bob had sent Ginger to assist Rosaline in getting ready for her most important day along with Evangeline of Evangeline's

Hair Salon.

There was also Miss White, the Home Ec. Teacher, who had assisted in altering a dress for Rosaline to accommodate her size. Woodlake didn't have many shops, and there was no time for Rosaline to order a dress from Sears. She was only able to find one dress in town that suited the purpose. It was a plain white dress and although originally tight, Miss White knew just what to do to made it fit to perfection. She had to rip a few seams, insert fabric from a bolt of lace she had kept in her closet for such a moment as this! She had been saving the lace for decades hoping to use it for her wedding one day, but she finally accepted the fact that might never happen and happily donated it to Rosaline. The dress was majestic, and Rosaline was quite pleased. The lace added an array of splendor.

Shoes were another story. She was adamant with the dress reaching to the floor, only the tips of her toes might stick out; and so she decided comfort was important on such a day as this. Contrary to wearing the heals that Lillian felt were more appropriate, Rosaline decided to wear her white, highly polished waitress shoes.

Evangeline pinned Rosaline's hair on top of her head with wispy tendrils hanging near her cheeks. She was attempting to assault Rosaline with hair spray from every angle, but Rosaline wouldn't have it, "Please, enough it's fine the way it is!"

Lilly had loaned Rosaline her veil, and Bob would be walking her down the aisle. The veil was sprinkled with tiny rhinestones, and it lightly covered Rosaline's face.

"Why all this fussing just for me," Rosaline thought embarrassed by all this attention.

In his apartment, Nathan Twitters was getting ready as well. He would be moving into Rosaline's home after today.

He had spent several weeks boxing up books and pictures, along with his high school and college diploma which had hung on his bare walls for years. He could fit most of his clothes into two suitcases that he kept under his bed, and Buzz had volunteered to drive his truck over to help move his belongings into Rosaline's. Nathan had gotten up very early to take his final look around his apartment that he had called home for over twenty years. He had packed most of his belongings over the week and given his landlord Mr. Hankins notice that he would be vacating the apartment by next week, allowing him a little time to clear it out, and tidy it up as he had found it when he had originally moved in. He also invited Mr. Hankins to their upcoming wedding.

Nathan thought that it being summer they might go on a honeymoon; yet for now, just getting used to living together would be enough for the two of them.

This day was difficult and wonderful for him, all at the same time. He loved Rosaline and was anxious for two o'clock to arrive. He knew he would need time to adapt to being a couple, but he felt ready. His mother would be attending, and she had given him her mother's gold band to place on Rosaline's hand during the ceremony.

"This is for you," she pushed it across his kitchen table, a small brown box stuffed with tissue paper. "It was my mother's and now I think you should give it to Rosaline." He didn't know what to say, as he opened it gently. It had tiny ruby chips set into the gold band and was quite large.

"My grandmother must have had large hands, like Rosaline, thank you," Nathan said, "it will be perfect."

His mother just nodded. She had held on to this ring for decades and although it was not in her nature to part with such a treasure as this, she wanted Nathan to have it. He was her only son and she loved him, even if at times she couldn't show it.

The diner's ovens were ablaze and for the first time in over thirty years a "Closed for the Day" sign hung out front. Everyone was headed to the church at two and would jam themselves into the diner afterwards for the celebration to follow.

The high school kids had helped with the decorations all morning. They had strung crepe paper flowers of every color throughout. There were jelly glasses on each table and in every booth and along the counter the jars were full of freshly cut daisies and tulips. Small votive candles were waiting to be lit. It would be a grand event. Over the diner's front door, a banner, created by the high school art department, swung in the breeze heralding the marriage of Nathan and Rosaline.

"It's almost time, we better leave", Rosaline anxiously blurted out. "It is happening, truly happening, let's get going."

As they stepped out the front door, Rosaline had a huge surprise waiting for her. There was Bob, who stood outside Rosaline's front door with a large hay wagon, he had rented, decorated in red and pink carnations. He jumped down and escorted Rosaline to sit next to him to travel the three blocks to the church. Bob was even wearing a blue suit and tie, another surprise for Rosaline.

Next, Buzz pulled up in his red truck to take Ginger, Evangeline and Miss White over to the church. It was a tight squeeze, but they happily fit.

As the large horses clopped along the streets Rosaline tried not to cry, she had wanted very much not to have her make-up run down her face, but this was all so overwhelming. Bob tried to comfort Rosaline and guide the horses easily along the street as many onlookers waved.

Finally, she arrived at the church and all the town's people had lined up to watch Rosaline step inside to begin the big event. As Rosaline was gently led off the wagon, Buzz rounded the corner and Ginger, Miss White and Evangeline jumped out to escort her inside for a final touchup. There in all her splendor, the girl who never fit in and always felt alone, was Roseline, Queen for a Day, just like the television show.

Inside the church, no one had seen Mr. Twitters. The crowd was wondering if he had changed his mind. "I wonder where Nathan is hiding? Do you think he got cold feet?" Gossip was flying.

At 12:30 PM, Rosaline was pacing in the church's rectory and adjusting her veil. Ginger tried calming her down. "I promise you Rosaline it will be fine. Everyone has the jitters on their wedding day," reacting to her nervousness.

Nathan was still nowhere to be seen. Still, no one dare tell Rosaline.

At 1:30 people started arriving at the church which was draped in pink and gold streamers between each pew. At the front of the church were two huge flower arrangements that Mayor Peeps had donated. The organist, Miss Bloom, was gently playing as the church began filling up. Reverend Jones was at the door welcoming everyone, while his brother, Officer Jones, was directing traffic and assisting the cars onto the grass.

There was Carmen Thompson who had taken off her gym sneakers especially for this day and her daughter Carmela. The Girls, Mary, Irene and Shirley, always together. They wouldn't have missed this for the world. Buzz, who ran home to change after dropping off the ladies, cleaned up quite nicely. He looked for Mary and squeezed in next to her. Toby Lester and her family were seated up front. Mrs. Brown, Nathan's third grade teacher, was honored to be invited. Mr. Henkins, his landlord, grinning from ear to ear, "Nathan's leaving the nest at last," speaking to anyone who would listen.

With only fifteen minutes to spare, Lilly n' Bob rushing into the rectory to tell Rosaline that they had arrived. Lilly ogled over how lovely Rosaline looked in her veil and how the dress fit perfectly. She handed her a bouquet of white and red roses with a large satin bow, chosen especially for her.

"Rosaline you look like a princess, Bob will steady you down the aisle. I'll go and sit down. One of the boys from the photography club at Woodlake High is out there and will take pictures. We thought of everything. The diner is glowing, too." Lilly told her, her maternal instinct in full gear.

Turning to Bob, "Bob," Rosaline softly spoke, "I'm scared."

"Take my arm and hold on tight, you'll be fine," Bob assured her, smiling proudly at his dear Roseline.

"Oh, here's a blue handkerchief," Lillian said, "You must carry it with you. Tradition, you know!"

At last it was two o'clock. Miss Bloom started playing beautiful music to quiet the large, packed hall. The traditional, Here Comes the Bride sweetly blared throughout the church. Everyone turned as Bob gallantly led Rosaline down the aisle and every head turned as John, President of Woodlake's Camera Club flashed away each step. Rosaline was blushing.

People began whispering again about the absence of Mr. Twitters. He didn't seem to be anywhere. Yet, at the exact moment Rosaline reached the end of the aisle-- up popped Nathan Twitters, wearing a grey tweed suit and flashy red tie that Rosaline had picked out for him at Porter's Department Store in the next town over. At the time, Nathan wondered if he would ever wear it again, now he knew this was perfect for such a day as this. He felt like a king looking into the eyes of his queen.

Nathan was anxious, but somehow unafraid as to what his life would suddenly become. No close friends nor many contacts, other than his students, he knew finding Rosaline was going to be fine. More than fine. Just then, his mom walked towards him and awkwardly hugged him, whispering softly, "I love you," and sat down. A huge sigh of relief reverberated among the guests. No one was sure how he arrived, but there he was standing perfectly straight and proud.

Rosaline looked into his eyes and he into hers. Neither seemed to take note of the church filled with welcoming onlookers. Nathan's mom, who rarely showed public emotion, was sniffling away, as was Lilly and many others in the hall.

Finally, "You may kiss the bride" echoed in Nathan's ears, realizing at that moment that they were in fact husband and wife at long last.

Nathan gave Rosaline a quick peck on the mouth and couldn't stop gazing into her eyes and being in awe of her beauty. Neither could let go of one another's hand, as they were ushered into a car to await their guests at Bob's Diner.

It was a celebration that no one ever forgot in the town of Woodlake. The overflow waited patiently outside on the stairs and upon folding tables surrounding the diner. People kept coming to the diner from late afternoon to midnight, sharing stories, bringing gifts, and showering love on the newlyweds who sat at a special table strewn with rose petals.

Lots of juicy burgers, shakes of all flavors, and baskets of French fries overflowed. There were cups of nickels available for guests to take and spin any selections they deemed suitable on the juke boxes.

It is rumored that Rosaline and Nathan Twitters had the best wedding that Woodlake had ever seen in all its history. The couple never stopped grinning at one another. A picture was snapped of the two newlyweds that forever hung-up front of Bob's Diner. It was said that it remained there for years to come. Possibly, forever.

Chapter 35

Hot, So Hot in Woodlake

ot in Woodlake once again. Schools out. Summer has arrived. Sprinklers turned on. Children running through cool sprays of water. The sounds of the droplets spraying forward and back can be heard on every block. Giggles echoing through the town as the heat envelopes the entire community. Folding aluminum chairs are brought out of garages, along with rusted barbeque grills, beach floats, plastic buckets and shovels still encrusted with sand from last summer's excursions. Toby, barefooted in shorts and a t-shirt, runs outside to greet the day. The morning sun has barely peeked through the clouds and already the oppressive heat has taken its toll.

Nearby, Bob's Diner begins filling up with customers looking for a tall glass of lemonade or a large Coke filled with ice. Regina Springer, newly arrived in Woodlake, briskly walks into Bob's, with her new pink gingham pedal pushers and crisp white off the shoulder top and bouffant hairdo teased to the sky. She swings open the doors and plops herself down at the counter. She appears to be in her twenties and very talkative.

"Hi," she blurts out to Bob and anyone who will listen, "I'm Regina Springer and I just moved here to Woodlake. I can type 70 words per minute. I graduated from Bricktown's Secretarial School with a 80% average. Do you know anyone looking for a good secretary?"

Bob whose back was to Regina, quickly turned around. "Why, welcome. You were saying? I wasn't paying much attention. I was setting up the sides." "I am looking for a secretarial job, and I'd like a very large Coke please, with lots of ice," she said in one breath.

As the large wooden ceiling fans were whirling around, conversation needed to be heightened. Almost screaming this time Regina repeated her mantra, "I am looking for a secretarial job." With the volume amped up a few decibels, Bob finally responded, "Welcome, to Woodlake. You're new? You've picked a good place to begin your job hunt, everyone will eventually wind up in here today to cool down. I will make sure to get the word out." Rosaline hoovering nearby overheard the conversation and with pad in hand, asked, "Anything to go with that large Coke? A burger, some fries?" Regina turned quickly towards Rosaline and just shook her head no, and with that Rosaline left to return with the drink.

The diner began to fill up with the heat wave on everyone's lips. Rosaline and Ginger kept the sodas flowing and fresh lemonade was a cool second. "Why one could fry an egg on the sidewalk, I heard they will be opening the Woodlake Pool tomorrow, before July 4th this year." Regina couldn't get over how the diner went from a low drown to a cacophony of conversations. She scanned the tables and counter and intuitively knew that today was the day she would find a job.

As she was deciding in which direction to go, a gangly young gentleman, hair flying in every direction, plopped onto the stool next to her and reached over the counter with familiarity to fill his glass with water. He couldn't wait for Rosaline or Ginger, the sweat was dripping down his temples, and his ravenous thirst couldn't last another moment. "Wow, you are thirsty, no doubt, my name is Regina Springer, I'm new in town." Thyus stared at Regina. As he gulped down the water, he scanned her face. He didn't say a word, just reached again for his second glass of water.

A little louder, this time Regina almost shouting, "My name is Regina Springer!" At that moment Rosaline rounded the counter, "He's hard of hearing, got kicked in the head last year at the annual touch football game." Rosaline turned to face Thyus and loudly spoke, "Do you want the usual?" He shook his head yes and once again Rosaline left, flying through the kitchen doors. Regina was embarrassed but tried to act normal.

She began to stare at the ceiling and then down at her Coke. Thyus had never seen such an attractive young woman in Woodlake, "Hey, it ain't nothing, if you just speak up I can understand most things". Regina began to relax, and started to chatter, "I am looking for a secretarial job? I just moved here." "Slow down," Thyus chuckled. With halting, but clear words, Thyus smiled, "I just took a break from my dad's office, and it just so happens that there is an opening. After I finish my lunch, I will introduce you." Regina almost tumbled off her stool, how could this happen. She hadn't even completely unpacked her suitcase at the Woodlake Y and maybe she might get her first job. Her Aunt Betty had always told her, there was no such thing as coincidences, things were just meant to be. She continued to shout in the direction of Thyus, "Why sure, I would love that. I'd better go home to change?" "No, you look fine." Thyus didn't want her to go. He had already decided that his dad must hire her on the spot.

Thyus sat up straight on the stool, tried to press down his unruly hair and quickly ate his juicy hamburger and fries, inviting Regina to share with him, and she complied, ravenously devouring most of it. After arriving in Woodlake and paying her month's rent at the "Y", there was very little left over for food. This was surly a sign, that today was her day.

When the last French fry was gone, Thyus paid and left his tip for Rosaline, as he always had done in the past, but things were not done as they always were in the past-- Thyus held out his arm to escort Regina out of the diner and he made sure to hold open the wide swinging doors, as well. Together, Rosaline, Ginger and especially Bob noticed that Thyus had an especially quick gait to his step which they had never witnessed before. That was surely a delight to see, especially on such a humid, stifling, hot, hot day in Woodlake.

The Epilogue

Fall leaves, winter snow, spring flowers and summer heat. Bob forever watched all his customers from the window of his kitchen as the seasons continued to repeat themselves. Bob's Diner remains nestled among the New Jersey pines and is forever a vessel of souls who have entered its large wooden doors. Within the tattered red booths, stories have attached themselves to the Formica table tops and into the grooves of the juke box records that continually spin round and round.

Bob met Lillian, now decades ago, as she innocently sat down next to him in his elementary classroom and then again in the diner as he was playing outside on the entrance way while his father worked tirelessly in the kitchen assisting his grandfather. There was Rosaline looking for part-time work while in high school and found a loving family in the walls of Bob's Diner. Twenty years later, Mr. Twitters would sit down at the counter asking for his toast buttered on both sides and be unaware how his life would forever become entwined with the talkative waitress that opened his heart to love. Toby a young girl finding her way in life, slurping down chocolate shakes to help her find solace in the difficult path of growing up. People were continuously interconnecting within a diner. A familiar diner. An ordinary diner. A special diner.

"Hey, Buzz can you help me get the cat out of the tree?" "Mr. Wright are you still teaching?" "Carmela, did you grow up happily?"

"I wonder where Father Bitner has gone?" "Did they ever find the killer of Ronnie's mom?" Questions floated in the air. Bob's Diner forever lived in the hub and hearts of Woodlake, New Jersey. As time travels forward, we remember other stories to share, other moments that catch our memories. New characters, and new tales.

And one day finally driving out of Woodlake down County Line Road, heading north you might look briefly over your shoulder to see that Bob's Diner is still there. You might still see that flashing pink sign heralding us to go inside to sit down for a while.

"Open," still flashing out its welcome, in pink neon, for all to see. Bob's Diner forever waiting to welcome you home, to hear your stories, still waiting to be told.

The End

Young Author Ellen T. Leeds (circa 1965) at home in New Jersey.

The Author

Ellen T Leeds, AKA Ellen Kaplowitz, grew up in New Jersey and now resides in Florida. She taught reading to adults, in a public vocational school in Miami, for over 30 years. She has always treasured books, writing, crafting, singing, and people. She lives with her husband Zooey and their two dogs. Their son and daughter-in-law live close by. Family is Ellen's number one love.

Several of her short stories appear in the books the *Red Bikini* and *Beyond My Window*.

Bob's Diner is Ellen's first novel.

Stay in touch with Ellen T. Leeds at
www.EllenTLeeds.com